"THIS MAY BE EDGERTON'S BEST NOVEL."
—*Newark Star-Ledger*

"Pitch the revival tent and sing hallelujah! Clyde Edgerton has returned to Listre . . . and for his legions of fans, that's cause for rejoicing. . . . *Where Trouble Sleeps* features an array of the wonderfully human, often quirky characters we've come to expect. . . . As always, Edgerton skewers the hypocritical and sanctimonious with hilarious deftness. . . . Beneath the comic flourishes lies a tender, bittersweet view of the world. Edgerton has given us small-town men and women in all their human frailty and splendor."

—*Charlotte Observer*

"Side-splittingly funny . . . Clyde Edgerton is the love child of Dave Barry and Flannery O'Connor. . . . He approaches O'Connor's dark view of human nature often, but in the end he serves up a lot more humor than she does. Just when it looks as though tragedy is going to be the blue-plate special, the laughs start arriving by the skilletful, a fresh batch on every page."

—*Raleigh News and Observer*

"Rollicking . . . Newcomers and old-time followers alike should . . . delight in his latest slice of small-town Southern life."

—*Southern Living*

"When Edgerton's debut novel *Raney* came out, I was impressed by how clever he seemed, how clearly and completely he was able to inhabit a voice, keep a joke running. Seven novels later, Edgerton hasn't lost that ability to capture a character, a tone, or a situation, but *Where Trouble Sleeps* is surely a superior, more mature work—clear evidence of his amazing growth as a writer. Without sacrificing humor, Edgerton has delved deeper into his characters; he takes what might have been simply funny or even ridiculous and reveals levels and layers of emotion, pathos, and even darkness. Amusing, engrossing, and insightful, *Where Trouble Sleeps* is a sublime achievement."

—*The Spectator* (Chapel Hill, NC)

Please turn the page for more rave reviews. . . .

The Blinker Light in Listre — 1950

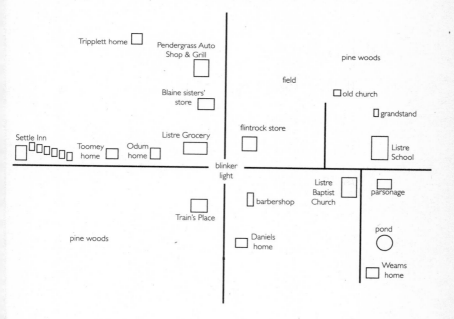

Clyde Edgerton

WHERE TROUBLE SLEEPS

a novel

BALLANTINE BOOKS
NEW YORK

A Ballantine Book
Published by The Ballantine Publishing Group

Copyright © 1997 by Clyde Edgerton
Reader's Guide copyright © 1998 by The Ballantine Publishing Group, a division of Random House, Inc.

Parts of this novel appeared in slightly different form in *The Oxford American*, *The Carolina Quarterly*, and *Best American Short Stories, 1997*.

http://www.randomhouse.com/BB/

Library of Congress Catalog Card Number: 98-96538

ISBN: 0-345-42632-0

This edition published by arrangement with Algonquin Books of Chapel Hill, a division of Workman Publishing Company.

Text design by Bonnie Campbell
Cover illustration by Christopher Zacharow

Manufactured in the United States of America

First Ballantine Books Edition: November 1998

10 9 8 7 6 5 4 3

*The fundamental order of ideas is first a world of things in relation,
then the space whose fundamental entities are defined by means of
these relations and whose properties are deduced from the nature of
those relations.*

—Alfred North Whitehead

*We had to live united with a wild beast whom it was important not
to know.*

—François Mauriac

CONTENTS

PART I

Summer Rain at the Blinker Light

SEND ME TO THE ELECTRIC CHAIR

ALEASE TOOMEY SAT at her dresser, putting on lipstick, getting ready to take her son up to see the electric chair for the first time. She blotted her lips on a Kleenex, reached for her comb. Her dresser top held the basics only—a jar of Pond's cold cream, a bottle of Jergens lotion, Elizabeth Arden rouge and lipstick, hand mirror, hairbrush—all on a starched white table doily.

She thought about little Terry Daniels, just down the road. Why not take him along, too? Seeing the electric chair might be especially good for him, and certainly his mother wouldn't be taking him up there. And it would be nice for Stephen to have some company along.

She blotted her lipstick again on the Kleenex, softened the glare.

≈

TERRY'S MOTHER, INEZ, squinted through the door screen. As Mrs. Toomey explained the purpose of the trip, Inez considered the dress Mrs. Toomey was wearing, a clean white dress with big blue flowers. Mrs. Toomey's hair was shiny and had nice waves in it, and little Stephen was so neat, wearing pressed navy blue shorts and a yellow shirt with a collar, his hair pushed back in front with that butch wax it looked like. She didn't have Terry's pants ironed. But he had some that was clean. Somewhere back in there.

As Mrs. Toomey talked, Inez began to realize that what Mrs. Toomey was about to do was exactly right for Terry at this time in his little dragged-along, up-and-down life. Her hand touched the screen. She looked over her shoulder and said, "Terry, go get on some pants and shoes. Find some clean pants and a shirt." Boy would go naked to the grocery store if he had a chance. She'd done blistered his ass twice for running naked in the yard. Last time was yesterday when she saw him standing on that tire, pissing in the hole.

"We'll just wait out here in the swing," said Mrs. Toomey.

IN THE SWING, Stephen sat next to the wall and held his mother's hand. His feet didn't reach the porch floor. The chain creaked up at the ceiling. He looked across the hot paved road at the gas station——Train's Place. He knew to take his eyes ·

away. Train's Place was where men drank beer and said bad words. Stephen knew the evil names of two beers: Schlitz and Blatz.

Through the window screen near his elbow he saw the foot of a bed, a rumpled white sheet. He'd never seen an unmade bed in the daytime. The unmade bed made the room seem wild. He heard Mrs. Daniels's voice in there: "Where's 'at other sock?"

"I 'on't know."

"Didn't you have it on yesterday?"

"No."

"Do you want me to whup you?"

"No."

"You say No ma'am."

"No ma'am."

"You say No ma'am to Mrs. Toomey, you hear? She's taking you up to see the electric chair, and you listen to what she says and don't you take them shoes off, or nary piece of your clothes . . . Do you hear?"

"Yes . . . Yes ma'am."

As they got in the car, Terry's sister, Cheryl, rode up on her bicycle, leaned it against the steps, and waved to Mrs. Toomey and Stephen.

The way Cheryl was shaped all over, the way her head and

5

her body came together like an angel, made her look to Stephen like the woman who came to him when he was almost dead on the desert after he'd been fighting Indians. Cheryl sometimes talked to him when he sat on the porch steps at the grocery store. She would sometimes even sit down beside him.

ALEASE LET STEPHEN and Terry sit in the backseat together. That way they could talk, and she could kind of hear what they talked about.

"Did you know Mr. Jacobs's got a electric paddle in his office?" Terry asked Stephen.

"Terry honey," said Alease, "I don't think that's true about a electric paddle. I think somebody made that up."

"That's what Leland said."

"Well, I don't believe that's true. That's a rumor. A rumor is something that's not true. Not usually true."

Stephen rolled his little metal car up and down his leg and across the seat.

"Can I play with that?" Terry asked Stephen.

Alease looked in the rearview mirror. "Stephen. Let Terry play with your car."

The strong, acrid odor from the fertilizer factory came in through the open windows.

Stephen handed his toy car to Terry and said, "I got about five more."

They bumped over the railroad tracks, past a row of shotgun houses, some with flowers on the porch.

"I got a big wood one," said Terry. "Leland's got a real one with wheels on it that come offen a scooter."

They drove past the Dairy DeeLight—where June Odum, a neighbor, worked part-time. Alease decided they might stop by on the way back for a little reward if Stephen and Terry behaved. She wasn't against a little reward for herself, either.

"Now, the reason we're going to see the electric chair," said Alease, "is so you-all can see what will happen if you ever let the Devil lead you into a bad sin. They'll put you in the electric chair and electrocute you. And little sins can lead up to big sins."

They drove past red clay road banks, past green pastures with cows, wood outbuildings, fishing ponds, some pastures holding a line or two of thick black-green cedar trees. They passed a man in a dark gray business suit changing a flat tire.

JUST EAST OF Birmingham, Alabama, big splotchy raindrops hit the dusty windshield of a northeast-bound, black, four-door, almost new, stolen 1950 Buick Eight. Jack Umstead looked for the wiper knob, found it. He was very satisfied

7

with the feel of this big Buick. The horn sounded like it weighed a hundred pounds. He kept patting the dashboard, and when he'd stopped for coffee in the sunshine, before the rain started, he had walked around the front of the car and touched the chrome hood ornament. It was shaped like a rocket ship. The heavy wipers worked with a clean, wide sweep—wider than any he'd ever seen—and at two speeds, fast and slow. He needed the fast. In fact, it was raining so hard he might pull over and stop for a few minutes. He didn't need a wreck, and the nose of some highway patrolman sticking in his window.

BACK AT THE blinker light, Inez sat in her big soft chair inside the house where she could look out from the comfortable darkness. She picked up her L&M from the ashtray. She liked to sit in her big chair and prop her feet on the cane-bottomed chair, with her smokes, matches, and ashtray on the little round table beside her. She liked to look out through the screen door from back in there where it was dark. She liked to watch the men over at Train's Place, drinking beer and talking. Beyond that she could see what was going on over at the grocery store.

Sometimes she went back to bed. She didn't like to cook especially and they didn't have company anymore now that Johnny had started drinking again. So sometimes she just gave up and slept. She deserved it. She'd had a hard time keeping her family going, except for Cheryl, who had made it all the way through high school and was turning out all right. She hadn't heard from her oldest son, Todd, in months. He was somewhere in Memphis, working at a gas station, he'd said.

AS THEY PULLED in and parked, Stephen's mother said, "See how big the building is? That's because there's so many prisoners."

Stephen looked at the tall fence beside the walkway—with barbed wire along the top—at the giant brick building, bigger than the hospital, sitting below a quiet blue sky with moving clouds so white they almost hurt his eyes. He reached for his mother's hand.

"See up there?" she said. "If they try to escape, that guard will shoot them. That's a shotgun he's got."

Stephen knew a gun would shoot an Indian and they'd fall down before they had a chance to go scalp a white man. He'd never seen a scalping close up in a movie. He wondered what it looked like up close. Did they get every bit of the hair, or just a hunk from the top? Why did that *kill* you? Why didn't a big scab just come?

The guard at the double gate said, "Yes ma'am. What can I do for you? Hey there, boys."

9

"I'm Mrs. Harvey Toomey. I called ahead to see about y'all showing these boys the electric chair."

"Oh, yes ma'am. We got a note about that." He opened one large gate, then another. "Just push the buzzer at that second door and Buddy'll let you in. How old are you boys?"

"Seven and a half," said Terry.

"Six and a half," said Stephen.

"This one's mine," said Alease. She touched Stephen's head.

These men in uniforms, Stephen knew, found lost dogs, fed milk to babies. On the outside—in their faces—they looked kind of hard, but inside they were perfect. They were prison guards. Maybe he'd be a prison guard when he grew up, stand up there in that high room at the top of the fence and hold a shotgun all day long and then go home to his wife for a good supper. And if he got in a fight with the prisoners and got shot, his beautiful wife dressed in white would rush to him, kneel over him, take care of him and talk to him. She would rub his forehead with a damp, white cloth.

AFTER THE BOYS and mother were gone, the tower guard asked down to the gate guard, "What'd she say?"

"Show them boys the electric chair." He shook a Lucky Strike up out of a pack, lit it with a flip-top lighter that had a rising sun on the side. "They won't but six and s'em year old."

"I wish I'd brought Dennis up here once a year or so from the time he was about two years old. Maybe he'd a stayed in school and made something out of hisself."

"You can't ever tell. When'd he drop out?"

"Eleventh . . . tenth. Somewhere in there. I think he made it to the eleventh in some subjects. He never did get a chance to play football because he couldn't get up to a damn C average."

"That's a rule that never made no sense to me. What the hell difference does it make what your average is if the only thing you know how to do is play football?"

"Yeah. Well, that was pretty much Dennis's story. Still is. He's thirty-one years old and the only thing he still knows how to do as far as I know is play football. But it's doing him less and less good, I'll tell you that."

"He still driving the drink truck?"

"Yeah."

"He can do that, can't he?"

"Oh yeah."

"Well . . ." The guard took a draw, blew smoke. "A man needs a skill."

"Yeah. That's for sure. But I'll tell you one thing: Some skills are better than others."

"Well, yeah, that's true. That's true."

INSIDE THE PRISON, a guard led Stephen, his mother, and Terry through a big metal door, several other doors, and finally to a thick door with an eye-level window about the size of a saltine cracker box.

"You boys come on over here and I'll show you the switch first. My name's Sergeant Floyd." Stephen noticed that he walked with a big limp. "Here it is. Now. There's the white, which is off. The green means ready. And the red is zap. Now the executioner can't see the prisoner from here, you see. Here, stand on this stool."

Stephen looked, saw a chair made of dark shiny wood, not as big as he thought it would be, on a low platform. Straps hung to the chair arms and legs and a light-colored canvas bag hung from the top of the chair back.

His mother looked over his shoulder.

"What's that bag?" he asked.

"That's what they put over his head," said Sergeant Floyd, "so you can't see his face when he gets fried. That's something you don't want to see."

"Let me see," said Terry.

"Let's let Terry see," said Stephen's mother. She placed her hands under Stephen's arms and lifted him down.

Terry stepped up, looked in through the window. "Where's the electric paddle?" he said.

"Oh, they just got them at school," said Sergeant Floyd. He looked at Stephen's mother and winked. "Now, this chair though—our bad people up here use this chair twicet . . . first time and last time." He looked at Stephen, winked again.

Stephen pictured an electric paddle—something shiny metal about the size of a lawnmower set up on the corner of a big desk. You bent over in front of it and a metal paddle hooked to the side of it went *rat-tat-tat-tat-tat* about a hundred miles an hour.

"I don't think you can teach them too soon," said his mother.

INSIDE THE DAIRY DeeLight, Alease saw June Odum waiting behind the serving window. She wore a little white Sealtest ice cream hat. It seemed as if June's big sad face—as round as the moon, with dark bags beneath her eyes—filled up the entire little window.

"How y'all?" said Mrs. Odum. Her whole body, everything about her, seemed sloped downward somehow—lines out from her eyes and her mouth, her shoulders, all sloped downward.

"Just fine, June. How you doing today?" Alease placed her purse on the counter. "Y'all go on over and sit down, son."

"Oh, I'm doing all right, I reckon," said June.

"We want to order three banana splits. These boys have been real good today."

June pulled three bananas from a bunch in a fruit bowl and began her work. She picked up her lit Pall Mall from a MIAMI FLORIDA ashtray and took a draw. The cigarette tip brightened, then dimmed. She moved slowly, as if she were underwater. She made the little grunting sounds she always made while she worked. "Where y'all been? Mmph."

"We been up to see the electric chair."

"Oh?"

"I don't think you can start teaching them too young."

"About . . . electricity?"

"About right and wrong."

"Oh, yes . . . mmph." Hard vanilla ice cream curled into the dipper. "Well, one thing for sure—you just can't beat the electric chair for putting a mean man to death. That gas is too easy."

June smoked and worked, and in a minute she placed three banana splits in the window opening.

"Oh, my."

At the table, Stephen asked, "What do prisoners get to eat?"

"They eat bread and water. Maybe a few vegetables."

"Can a prisoner be a Christian?"

"Yes, but that would be hard. Anybody who accepts Jesus as their saviour is a Christian."

"So there might could be a prisoner in heaven?" A speck of whipped cream stuck to Stephen's lower lip. Alease wiped it off with her napkin.

"That's right. But there probably wouldn't be many."

Two soldiers came in and ordered chocolate milk shakes.

"Are they in the army?" asked Terry.

"Yes," said Alease. "The army has the brown uniforms. The navy has the blue."

"Has the war started?"

"I'm afraid so. But this one won't be so big, I don't think."

STEPHEN SAW A Jap in his mind, the one in the movie. He came up from behind the silver napkin thing that you could pull a napkin right out of. He looked like a mad wasp, with slanted eyes, and he was yellow, and up behind him in the dark came a Korean. Stephen couldn't see what the Korean looked like. Maybe a little bit like a stalk of corn. Something with lightning in his eyes.

One of the soldiers asked his mother, "Is there any stores on down the road?"

"If you keep going on down that way you'll come to a blinker light and there are three or four stores around there."

"We need some supplies."

ALEASE AND HARVEY sat at their kitchen table next morning. They had sausage, scrambled eggs, toast, orange juice, and coffee. Alease was feeling a slight regret at not mentioning the electric chair trip to Harvey.

"I want you to build a flower bed there beside the garage," said Alease. "I think you can do it with posts for the two corners and then fill it in with some topsoil and mulch."

"I'll look at it, see if I can't get some posts from behind the store or Papa's smokehouse."

Alease wondered when that might happen. "And then will you build it?"

"Yes. That's what I'm saying."

"Maybe Stephen could help you do a few little things."

"We'll see."

"I took him to see the electric chair yesterday—and Terry Daniels, too."

"Why'd you take Terry?"

"For the same reason I took Stephen. To let him see what happens if you break the law, commit a sin. Here, take this toast. I like it a little browner."

"I don't think I'd be taking other people up there—other children—I don't think."

"Why?"

"I just wouldn't. It seems like it's intruding."

"If his daddy had been taken up there when he was a boy, he might not have turned out like he did."

"Well, I just feel like it might be a little bit getting in their business."

"I stopped by there and asked Inez." Alease cut a sausage link with her fork. "I wish you could have gone with us." She chewed. "That store is taking a lot of time lately it seems like." He was out there just about every morning before work, nights after work, sometimes at lunch or when he'd get a half-day off, most Saturdays — the last three or four — and then he'd be so tired he'd sleep most of Sunday afternoon.

"Well . . . Steve ought to be back sometime today."

"It looks like to me he could have waited till tomorrow to go fishing. Since he don't go to church anyway."

"It takes more than one day."

"At least I wish he'd get somebody else to help out some of the time. You've got a job."

"He can't afford it yet. But I think he'll be able to before too long."

Alease poured herself some more coffee.

"I do things with y'all," said Harvey. "And I'm teaching him to play baseball." Harvey sipped his coffee. "I got to get on down there. I'll leave the car here."

"I'd like for all three of us to do something some Saturday maybe. You hadn't had a whole Saturday clear in I don't know when."

"Alease, I'm helping out Steve. I have to help out my brother. He needs a little help, that's all. You don't expect me to just sit by when I can be helping him out, do you?"

"No. But you've got a family. Here, in this house."

"I know that."

STEPHEN AWOKE TO his mother's touch and voice: "It's time to get up, Stephen."

Stephen remembered. "Can we do Feed the Pigs?" He hadn't played that game in a long time.

"Are you sure? Aren't you a little too old for that?"

"No ma'am." This was the best game in the world.

"Here," she said. "Put these on—and this, then come on out on the porch."

He'd gone to sleep holding her hand, as he always did. He'd reached over from his bed to hers, and he awoke to her voice. Just before and just after sleep were times when nothing bothered him, scared him, hurt him, got after him, worried him. Before sleep was when she read him a story or two from *Aunt Margaret's Bible Stories,* and then they said their prayers. Some of the stories were scary sometimes.

He got out onto the porch as fast as he could, crawled up into the wooden swing, turned, and plopped down.

His mother sat facing the swing—eggs, sausage, and toast in a plate in her lap. She pushed the swing to get it going, stuck a bit of egg with the fork, gave the swing another little push.

"Come here, little pig," she said. She was looking out toward the road.

He looked too. Drops of dew reflected morning sunlight.

"Come here, little pig. I got you something to eat. You come on over here, now. Get you something to eat."

On his next swing forward Stephen mouthed the food.

His mother lowered the fork toward the edge of the porch floor. "Here you go, little pig." Gasp. *Why—what in the world happened to your food, little pig?"*

More egg, a bit of sausage. "Little pig, come here, little pig. I got you some good food this time. Here you go little pig . . . *Now, what . . . what in the world happened to your food, little pig?"*

Stephen saw his black kitty. "Inky just crossed the road," he said, chewing.

"He did? Well, I need to go get him. He'll get run over. Where did he go in the woods?"

"Right across from the mailbox."

"You got to help me keep an eye on him. He must've got out when I emptied the trash. He's your cat now and you've got to watch out after him like David—and Jesus—did with the sheep. When one little sheep didn't come home at night, they'd go out and look and look until they found him. They never gave up until they found the one lost lamb."

JACK UMSTEAD, DRIVING north in his Buick Eight, said to himself, "Rusty Smith, Rusty Smith, Rusty Smith." It was a name he hadn't used in a while. He was listening to Roy Acuff on the radio sing "Great Speckled Bird." It was just a real pleasure to drive this fine automobile.

He wondered how many people in the world said "automobile" and how many said "car." Probably divided about even. That was one of the things that *could* be known if there was just a way *to* know. There was a number of people who said "car"—a specific number—and a number who said "automobile," and a number who said both. Just like there was a number for the grains of sand on earth. Just no way to know all those numbers. And then there were things you couldn't know, like "why" things. Why was hot *hot* and cold *cold*— well, maybe that could be known, but it was more complicated. It wasn't just a number like the grains of sand. But even the number of grains of sand would probably be harder than that: figuring out what was a grain and what was a tiny rock. You'd have to do more than count.

After driving past and coming back from the other direction, he pulled into a place called Alligator Jimmy's Fried Catfish Eats. He always drove into and drove out of an establishment in the direction opposite to his real route of travel. Next door to Jimmy's was a little zoo there and a few other places of business across the road. He'd passed a motel within a mile. Two churches back there. He was just outside Atlanta, Georgia, and didn't see why he shouldn't stay here a few days if it felt right. Then if a particular store looked ripe, why, he'd relieve it before heading north.

Umstead, since he'd never heard the call to be a Christian, and couldn't come to believe he was supposed to hear it, had decided some time back that he would more or less live off the land. The one thing he *didn't* want to do was pretend *to himself* that he was a Christian, which as far as he could tell was what all Christians did except maybe one or two preachers he'd met. He didn't want no part of halfway.

"What can I get for you?" The man wiped the table with a wet-looking cloth. That had to be Alligator Jimmy.

"I'd like some breakfast. Two over easy, bacon crisp, grits, and toast."

The man turned and shouted to the kitchen, "Two over,

bacon, toast." He turned back to Umstead. "It was all crisp this morning. Coffee?"

"That's right. Black. Are you Alligator Jimmy?"

"Yep."

"My name's Rusty Smith and I'm just driving through from Columbia." They shook hands. "Some of my kinfolks used to live around here somewhere and I'm trying to track them down."

"Pleased to meet you, Rusty." Jimmy raised the rag and pointed. "Is that a Buick Eight you're driving?"

"Sure is. Mighty nice car. I like it a lot."

"I been threatening to buy a Chrysler. My daddy always wanted one. Went to his grave wanting one."

Umstead wondered whether or not he ought talk to this guy about something like cooking as a art or cooking as a science. He'd wait until after he got his food. "You only live once," he said.

Now, he didn't mind pretending he was a Christian to somebody *else*. That could be fun—if the situation was right.

BIG TOP GRAPE

EARLY IN THE afternoon, Stephen's mother walked him to the store to stay with his daddy for a while.

On the way, she said, "As soon as you see I'm walking next to the road, you trade places with me. A gentleman always walks next to the road in case a car splashes. Then it will get on the man and not the lady. Do you understand?"

"Yes ma'am."

"That's what a gentleman always does. Let's hurry. I want to get back before it storms."

Opal Register was pulling into her mother's driveway with her mother sitting beside her. They'd been shopping. Opal looked into the backseat. "Mother, where's your umbrella?" "Lord, I don't know." "We left it in one of those stores. Do you remember leaving it somewhere?" "There ain't no telling. There ain't no telling." "Well, try to think. I declare." "Well, don't get mad at me. You been everywhere I been." / Sylvia Roberts called out to her two boys, out under the woodshed. "You boys get in here. It's fixing to rain." / Beneath the blinker light, raindrops bounced like hail. Steam drifted along the asphalt; a fine mist sat still above the road. / Over at the flintrock store—a general merchandise store—a man holding a newspaper above his head ran beneath the drive-under shelter. Raindrops spread on his thin summer shirt, the wet making the skin show through. Several men stood under the shelter. A rush of cool air blew in. Rivulets began to run through orange clay, carrying tiny rocks, a cigarette butt. Gusts of wind scurried water across the ground. "That's a hard one." "You can't hardly get too much rain this time of year." "Well, you *can* get too much. You can drown things." "Well, I'll tell you one thing. You can't get hardly too much." "We might have to go in if that wind keeps up." Somebody farted. Everybody laughed. It was a good one. Well, hell, they all were. Fred

Jernigan chewed tobacco, stood, and spit out into the rain when the time came. One or two were stubble-faced from missed shaves. The Nehi man stood holding on to his delivery cart, eyeing his truck through the rain. Somebody told a nig-ger joke. No hard feelings, though—nothing said that could bring hard feelings to the surface. No talk about God or the universe. A word on politics, something about the communists in Chapel Hill. Some talk about MacArthur and the new war in Korea. A little talk about the atomic bomb, the Japs. Casey Odell pulled a long string to the bare lightbulb in the white-flaked tongue-and-groove ceiling of the drive-under. The wind picked up. Out over the intersection, the red and yellow blinker light reflected off the streaking rain, and a tiny chill ran through Casey, making the hair on the back of his neck stand up.

Stephen looked out into the rain from his seat on the bench at the grocery store. His legs swung back and forth. In his hand he held a Big Top grape drink, the bottle bottom on the bench beside him. It was raining too hard to sit out on the step.

Through the rain he watched the men over at Train's

Place stand around under the shelter and drink beer—the one store in the community that sold beer. The flintrock sold buckets and overalls and fishing poles; the grocery, groceries. The Blaine sisters' store sold ice and chickens mostly. The grill, hot dogs and hamburgers. And the auto shop fixed cars. Stephen had been inside all of them except for Train's.

Terry had told him about the inside over there, that it was dark, that Mr. Train sat behind the cash register in the dark in his wheelchair and fixed radios, that a calendar on the wall had a naked woman picture on it.

When just about anybody in Stephen's family went to the beach on vacation to stay in the Douglass cabin, they always stopped at Train's Place and filled up with gas. His daddy would go inside and come back with a twenty-dollar bill that Mr. Train had given him in case of trouble on the trip. He did that when people went on trips. Everybody always brought it back—something Stephen couldn't quite figure out. Why did people talk about that?

Mr. Train's brother, Mr. Luke, lived in a little short trailer right behind the service station. He was Mr. Train's mechanic. Mr. Blake, another brother, worked there most of the time. And there were some other brothers who came and went. The sign out front said REDDING BRO. GULF SERVICE STATION, TRAIN REDDING, PROPRIETOR. "Proprietor" was just some word. His mama showed him how to read it. But she wouldn't let him go over there, except when they stopped to get gas.

Behind Mr. Luke's trailer were big piles of old tires. One time they caught on fire and the smoke was black and jumped up rolling from flashing orange flames. Somebody hooked Mr. Luke's trailer to a truck and pulled it out of the way. The fire truck came, but didn't do anything. People stood around and watched. You could feel the heat all the way from over on the grocery store porch—like a hot cloth on your face. Some-body said Mr. Train had wanted them to burn up, and that's why the fire truck didn't put them out.

Stephen wondered why the church hadn't gotten mad at Train's Place and done something to it because of the beer-selling and -drinking.

PREACHER CRENSHAW, DOWN the road, sitting in his study, looked at the rain gusting against his window through the screen. He was thinking that maybe instead of sending $2,700 to the Lottie Moon offering they should just give it to somebody like Cheryl Daniels and a few other needy people. Cheryl was a girl who could go to college and make some-thing out of herself. Her family could use some money. And it really was a matter of money. It was a shame about the little bit of money they must have. With a thousand dollars they might buy a car and fix up that house. But somehow the idea of giving money to people in the community wouldn't work. It just wouldn't work. You had to give money to some organization far away. Think of all the money that had gone to somewhere in China.

Crenshaw closed his Bible, stood, walked over and looked out the window. He could see down to the blinker light. The whole end of his driveway was under water. What about poor people in the community, poor people within driving distance? What about those Negroes over in T.R.? Andrew, the church janitor, was from over there and the church did pay him a fair salary. That was the right thing to do. He'd supported fifty cents an hour, against the will of Mr. Clark and Mr. Sanders. And when he'd taken Andrew home one Thanksgiving eve and stopped nearby with some food for the Negro family that had lost two cousins in a car accident, he'd noticed a windowpane missing from beside the bed in the bedroom— so somebody could spit tobacco juice out the window, or that's what it looked like. He didn't know any white people who'd do that. But then again, just because he didn't know about it didn't mean it wasn't out there somewhere. In fact, what was so bad about spitting out the window? He turned and went back to his sermon. He was preparing Sunday's sermon on the power of the Trinity.

STEPHEN FELT SAFE on the grocery store porch. Around him were slat-wood baskets stocked with tomatoes, potatoes, onions, corn, turnips, turnip greens, cucumbers, and squash. The rain smell was strong, mixed with some raw vegetable, dirt smell. He turned up his Big Top grape, the only bottled drink he knew about besides a beer that had a long swelled neck. He dared to pretend he was one of them. But there was an understanding between him and the whole world that he should never go over there alone, never set foot in that place.

Terry said some men did their drinking over behind the candy counter inside Train's and that he'd seen Stephen's uncle Steve doing it, but Stephen knew Terry made that up. That could not be true. That was a lie. Sometimes Terry told lies. Leland did too. Leland Triplett. Leland's daddy, Mr. Triplett, was a beer drinker and a truck driver who stayed gone most of the time.

Inside the grocery store were more bins of vegetables, a counter and cash register, shelves of boxed goods. On the wall behind the cash register were cigarettes, aspirin, BC powders, and big cardboard posters holding combs, handkerchiefs, and socks. At least one red comb was always clothespinned to the top of the comb cardboard, and when a little boy of the community got old enough to get a haircut by himself, Big Steve said, "Hey, boy, you see that red comb up there? When you let Mr. Taggart cut your hair by yourself, I'll

29

give it to you. Free of charge. But you be sure you tell him to leave them sideburns. You hear?" And everybody always laughed. "Sideburns" was a mysterious word, too, and funny, because everybody laughed.

Behind the meat case in the back of the grocery were two table-sized chopping blocks, an electric meat grinder, and a hand-cranked slicer. Stephen loved to watch meat hunks go into the top of the grinder and then come out below, moving slowly like a bunch of thick red strings, falling onto waxed meat paper held by his daddy or Uncle Steve. Sometimes Uncle Steve would let him cut the switch on or off, but his daddy wouldn't. The year before, Stephen watched Big Steve walk from back there holding his hand in a white towel as blood dripped dark red from his elbow. He'd never seen blood like that, except from a hog or chicken. Stephen's daddy had asked Levi Parsons, the only customer at the time, to mind the store and watch Little Steve until he and Big Steve got back from the hospital. Over the days it took to heal, Big Steve would pull back the bandage every now and then and show Stephen the long stitched cut. But his other uncle's scar, his uncle Raleigh's scar, was the best one of all. His arm got shot off in World War I up above his elbow and right in the end of it was an X, and when Uncle Raleigh was so drunk he couldn't move, Stephen would stand and look at it and study the little dips and curves of that X and think about his mother saying Uncle Raleigh could sometimes feel the arm that wasn't there. He liked to hear his mother tell all about how it had happened, and about how Uncle Raleigh came home and couldn't ever get over it.

ACROSS THE WAY from Stephen, beyond the blinker light, Terry Daniels sat on his porch watching the rain. His house had a shallow porch, so he sat back up against the wall. The green metal porch chair had been moved around to the back-yard. Terry studied the ends of three rotting porch planks, their familiar ragged ends, looked through the rain at the grocery store porch, made out the red of tomatoes, the green of string beans. A cardboard box of kittens had been on that porch several weeks ago. Stephen's mama got Stephen one, a black one. They named him Inky. Terry's mama wouldn't let him get one. They already had cats all over the place. His sister, Cheryl, took care of them mostly. She talked to them and named them: Cindy, Doggie, Puddin, and Pirate. He thought maybe he'd like to kill one sometime. The Blaine sisters had a three-legged gray cat.

He watched the rain move along in sheets. Cabbage? Or was that collards over there? And Stephen. Stephen had everything in the world: car, grocery store. A mama that had nice dresses, fixed up her hair, took Stephen places in the car. He had screens on all his windows. He said he was going to heaven. Stephen was who Terry wanted to be sometimes — without Stephen's clothes and Stephen's kind of mean and clean mama — so that he would be sure he was going to heaven, and be able to ride in a car, and have a black kitten that would be just his, and not Cheryl's.

A Chevrolet pulled in at the Blaine sisters' store. A Chevrolet face had a turned-down fish mouth, and the rear end had little beady-eye taillights. A man in an overcoat got out, went to the store front door, tried to open it, got back in and drove off. He didn't know that when it stormed, the Blaine sisters got scared and drove to their sister's.

Lightning flashed, then cracked, thunder boomed, not all that far away. Mist drifted onto Terry's face.

His mother called out from inside, "Terry, get in here. I need you to do something for me."

"Can I go over to the grocery store and see Stephen first?"

"NO. HELL, NO." What the hell? Why the hell was he always wanting to do something? Why couldn't he just do what she said do? She needed a nap. She needed a cigarette. She shook one up from the pack.

Terry pulled the string from the overhead lightbulb.

"Turn out that damn light."

If she dropped ashes on herself she brushed them off and by the time they reached the floor they'd about disappeared.

BACK OVER AT the grocery, Stephen watched Casey Odell get out of his truck and hurry in from the hard rain. "Hey there, Little Steve." He headed on in the store, came back out with a pack of Luckies, sat beside Stephen, thumped the pack on the bench, opened it, pulled out a cigarette, and lit it with a stick match. Stephen had once seen Casey wearing his navy uniform with all the buttons.

Striking that match like he did, on the bench, and wearing a navy uniform was something Stephen could see himself doing when he grew up. Being in the navy and dressed up in that uniform and going somewhere on a ship would be just about one of the biggest things in the world. He looked at the cigarette between Casey Odell's fingers, thought about getting some candy cigarettes. Sticks of chalk they looked like, with the ends painted red. Sometimes an end almost got missed—just a tiny bit of red on it.

Casey grabbed Stephen's knee and pinched it. Stephen pulled away, smiling, holding his Big Top grape.

The rain pounded the ground and pavement. Casey's cigarette smoke made its way out into the rain as if flowing along an invisible riverbed. He said, "Tell you one thing—that is a hard rain. Huh, boy?"

"Yessir." Stephen looked at the side of Casey's kind of ugly face while Casey looked out into the rain. Big nose, thick glasses, frog eyes. He had a scar on his chin like the ones that Mr. Train had on his face from the mule-truck wreck. Stephen said, "If it'd been raining when Mr. Train was in that wreck maybe that would have washed off the mule stinky and glass."

Casey looked at Stephen, then stood. "Mr. Toomey," he called out, going inside, smoke flowing around his head like a boat wake, "you got a right smart boy out here. Guess what he just said. He said . . ."

Stephen was afraid about his daddy hearing that he'd just said "stinky." He turned up his Big Top grape. He'd wait and see if his daddy was a little bit upset, and if he wasn't, he'd ask for a pack of candy cigarettes. It said LUCKY STRIKE on the pack, too. His daddy worked at Liggett & Myers, where they chopped up tobacco and put it in cigarettes. He'd heard his daddy talk about suckering tobacco and tying tobacco when *he* was a little boy, and when Stephen's daddy took him to the homeplace he'd shown him the tobacco barns where he'd once spent whole nights tending the fires. The fire would be warm and in a little tunnel that went into the barn while his daddy slept in the cold outside near the heat, waking up to check the fire. His daddy had even said that he and Stephen and his mama might move to the farm. That way Stephen could have a horse or a mule and get to smell the horse smell and ride like Roy Rogers. Then he could pretend to kill Indians like a real cowboy on a real horse.

The rain suddenly let up some.

Stephen went inside and came back out with his pack of candy Luckies, opened it, pulled out a heavy chalk candy cigarette, pretended to light it from a pretend match struck on the bench, pulled both of his feet up, and crossed his legs beneath him. He held out the candy cigarette and practiced all the ways he knew of flicking off ashes. While he flicked he saw Terry Daniels, a black raincoat over his head and shoulders, run down his steps, splash to the edge of the road, look both ways, cross the road, walk among the men, and go inside Train's Place.

INEZ DANIELS WATCHED Terry go out into the rain and into Train's. She noticed the Toomey boy, Little Steve, sitting over there on the grocery store porch, smoking a . . . ? What the hell? His mama would wear him out. Oh . . . candy cigarettes. Yes.

If she herself had a job at a store or somewhere, then she could get cigarettes for half-price. She liked Kools, the way they iced down your mouth, and they were better for your health than other cigarettes. If she could get some half-priced she could save some money for a little more wine.

When they'd moved from her mama's house after her mama lost her mind and died, that blinker light liked to have drove her crazy, blink-red/blink-red/blink-red/blink-red day night day night day night day night. She'd had to nail towels over the bedroom window but you could still *feel* it flashing out there. It made red shadows, red shade. It got on her nerves.

"You'd think she'd go get her own wine." "Not over to Train's Place I don't think." "I'll tell you one thing. That's the one thing, I guess the only one thing that's stood in our entire family: You don't hit a woman." "Ours too. Most families. Most families that I know about. As far back as I know about, too." "There's one in every community, I guess." "Yeah, I guess so." "And not a thing you can do about it." "And you know normally, he's just as nice a man as he can be." "He is. And funny too. You know, he can say some funny things." "Look at that water coming out of that gutter over there. That's what you call raining."

CROSSING THE ROAD again, Terry held the bottom of the wet-getting-wetter paper bag like Mr. Train had told him so the wine wouldn't break through. He could feel cool water between his toes in his left boot. Inside Train's, Terry had seen Big Steve sitting over behind the candy counter in the dark drinking a Blatz. He'd seen the naked woman on the wall, and the pieces of a radio that Train had taken apart on the table over behind the counter.

LIGHTNING BLASTED IN the woods behind the grocery.

Stephen stood quickly and went inside. Hairs were standing up on his arms. He met Casey coming out. Casey patted him on the head.

Inside, he said, "Daddy, Terry went over to Train's Place and got some wine again."

"Oh?" His daddy was running leftover meat package string off one spool onto another.

Stephen was beginning to get some idea about who was going to hell and who was going to heaven. His mama and daddy and aunts and uncles were pretty clear. Terry's daddy —Mr. Daniels—was pretty clear: He was going to hell for getting drunk and yelling and beating up Mrs. Daniels. Mrs. Daniels was going to hell for drinking wine. He, Stephen, would go to hell if he didn't accept Jesus, something he was getting old enough to figure out to do. His mother said he was old enough. The preacher did, too. A lot of it—getting saved —had to do with visiting old people and going to church every time you were supposed to, cutting off the Blaine sisters' toenails, and things like that for old people. And not drinking beer and whiskey. And it had to do with not saying ugly words, not touching stinky, keeping your pants on, keeping quiet when you were supposed to, not running away from your mama, not playing with your doodie, eating what you were supposed to eat, drinking milk, and being quiet, and it definitely had to do with Moses, Jesus, Peter, Mary, Zacchaeus, Isaac, God, Joseph, Abraham, David, Adam, Ezekiel, Miriam, and not playing in the mud. And it had to do with the story about Stephen's grandmother when she one time whipped his mama for cutting a piece of cloth on the Lord's Day. And Stephen, the one who got stoned for believing in God. It had to do with him. Somebody got named after him and then went to World War I, and Big Steve was named after that one, and then when Big Steve went to World War II, Stephen got named after him.

And it had to do with saying your prayers: closing your eyes and seeing the white that was Jesus and then saying a prayer to it.

"I don't know," said his daddy. "I just don't know. Do you want to do some sweeping?"

"Yessir."

"Get the broom and sweep out behind the meat counter."
Stephen loved to sweep dirt into the dustpan, move it back,
sweep the line of dirt, move it back, sweep the line of dirt. It
was a grown-up thing.

HARVEY, HOLDING THE long-handled clasper, tipped a box
of cornflakes, brought it down, and then a box of Tide to take
home to Alease as soon as Big Steve came back from fishing.
He didn't want to forget. He looked out the door. The afternoon sun had come out, catching and holding drops of water
on the big sign at Train's Place.

A shotgun blast erupted from down behind the Blaine sisters' store. They were already back home after the storm —
and they'd killed another chicken. Miss Bea had twice called
Stephen over to let him watch her shoot. She might even let
Stephen shoot some chickens, she'd told Harvey. That would
be fun for him, and the little shotgun didn't hardly kick at all,
she'd said. It did the job just right.

ALLIGATOR JIMMY DIDN'T remember anybody he'd liked
as much as Rusty Smith, in a long time. For one thing, the
man knew a lot. He was a bit down on his luck and could use
the cot in Jimmy's office for a night or two. Jimmy liked to
help out people he liked. And if all turned out the way Jimmy

39

hoped it would, this Smith fellow just might be the one to run his cousin's little zoo next door. There was going to be a lot of potential for zoos the more people went on car trips. Smith recognized this, and had expressed interest in the zoo business. Jimmy's cousin was about ready to sell because he had to pay that big fine, and Jimmy was in a good position for a bank loan. Things were coming together.

CHURCH HOME

FRAMED PHOTOGRAPHS SAT on tables throughout Mr. and Mrs. Weams's small white-frame house near the far side of the church pond—photographs of their children on down through great-grandchildren mostly, and other relatives. If nothing happened, they'd have some great-great-grandchildren within a year or two. How wonderful it would have been if their parents were alive to see all this offspring.

Mrs. Weams had taken a heating pad over to Mrs. Clark in the church secretary's office to put on that sprained ankle. And the quad cane her daddy once had. And some food. And a radio. In spite of all Mrs. Clark's excited ways, Mrs. Weams couldn't help but like her. And she was such a good church secretary—a job that she must have been called to—in spite of all the medicine she took. And she and Mr. Clark seemed so very happy together, although there had always been some question about Mr. Clark owning all those Cadillacs one after another, and that big diamond ring.

"We're mighty lucky to have somebody as good as her to be the secretary," Mrs. Weams said as she turned back the covers on her side of the bed.

Mr. Weams, standing over in the corner, held on to the back of his chair, taking off his pants as best he could. "We sure are," he said. Sometimes he forgot whether he was putting them on or taking them off. He liked to tell the story about the two old maids: One upstairs needing help, standing naked, half in and half out of the tub, called out to her sister, who didn't come for the longest time—so finally she called out again, and her sister said she was on the stairs but couldn't remember if she was going up or down. "Come on up— you're coming up." When her sister finally got up there, the upstairs sister couldn't remember if she was getting *in* the tub or *out*. Mr. Weams liked to tell that story when he forgot something. He was telling it right often lately, and it was getting so he kept forgetting the story itself, which one time made him stop telling it right in the middle of telling it, which was a brand new story he told for a while—the story about forgetting the story, that is—along with the one about Lizzy Swanson. Lizzy's grandson visited from Tennessee and she hadn't seen him in over twenty years. He said, "I'm David, your grandson." She said, "Come on in for some cookies." Then once they sat down, she said, "Now who'd you say you were?" and he said, "*David,* your grandson. You remember your daughter Betty, don't you?" She said, "Yes, I remember Betty." He said, "Well, I am Betty's *son* and that makes me your *grand*son." And Lizzy leaned across the table, looked him in the eye, and said: "That's too deep for me."

Mrs. Weams continued, "And she didn't complain about that sprained ankle one time and it all swelled up the way it was."

"You took her something to eat?"

"Took her a egg salad sandwich and a piece of that apple pie. I would of took her some of the lemon pie but the meringue won't right and I kinda wanted the rest of that for us."

"Did she have all her medicines?"

"Lined up on a shelf in the bookcase where she could reach them from the couch. But I don't believe she's as nervous as they say. I've never seen her when she didn't seem like herself."

Mrs. Weams placed her hand on the bed and slowly turned to sit.

Mr. Weams did the same on his side.

"Dear Lord," she said, "we are gracious for Thy bountiful

love, and we ask for guidance in all we do and say. Bless Dorothea in her time of need. Be with her. Bless Mike, Nannie, Richard, and Jane, and all their children and grandchildren. We pray for the sick and afflicted, dear Lord, and we pray in Thy blessed name, amen."

"Dear Lord," prayed Mr. Weams, "we are indebted for Thy everlasting love. Watch over us, we pray, in all we do and say. Grant us the courage to face each day and to follow Thy commandments. May we all learn the place of God in our homes, and the place of love and obedience and steadfastness in our hearts. In Jesus' name, amen. No telling what would happen to the books, the accounting, if it wadn't for her."

Mrs. Weams rolled back and down into bed, as her husband did the same from his side. She missed bumping his head by about the same margin she had each night for sixty-three years, except for the nine months and twelve days at the end of World War I when he served in the army down in Rome, Georgia, and then up in Norfolk, Virginia. He never had to go overseas.

JACK UMSTEAD WAS driving north in his Buick Eight. He was seven hundred dollars to the good. Alligator Jimmy sold three bird dogs for two hundred dollars apiece at about 5 P.M. out in front of the store and brought the money inside.

44

Umstead watched him and found it plus another hundred, within the hour, in a cigar box. He hit the road after offering his good buddy Alligator Jimmy a hearty thanks for all his Georgia hospitality, and left him an address in case Jimmy got involved in the zoo business. It turned out that his Smith kinfolks were in Albany, Georgia, he told Jimmy, not Atlanta. He'd misread some information.

He'd headed south, but then circled and headed north again.

OVER IN HER church office, Mrs. Claude T. Clark, Dorothea, sat on the clean white sheet she'd tucked around the couch cushions. This was so comfortable. She felt within the very clean presence of the Lord Jesus. She'd taken all her capsules and was waiting on taking her little white pills so she could get some space between them and the capsules. She needed a little more space than she'd been getting. Claude T., bless his heart, had gotten every single bottle of her medicine to her.

But Claude T. was buying a new Cadillac every year. And, he'd bought a diamond ring for himself. She just didn't feel that that kind of behavior was of the Lord. But the Cadillacs made him so happy, gave him something to talk about, something to spend his time on. A Cadillac was way too much car for her, with automatic windows, automatic this, automatic that, and Claude T. paid somebody uptown to wash it every week, and they used a vacuum cleaner on the inside. He'd bring it home and you could see vacuum cleaner streaks in the carpet—it had carpet—and they'd still be there when he got it rewashed and revacuumed again the next week.

Dorothea was Mr. Clark's second wife. She had lived with her older sisters, Bea and Mae, under the store for all those years—her whole life before Mr. Clark's first wife, Lucinda, died of a heart attack and he asked Dorothea to marry him fourteen months later, twelve years ago, when she was fifty-eight.

How in the world she could go from fifty-eight to seventy in that short a time was what she wanted to know. There it was, just sitting there, twelve years gone. She'd been willing to marry Claude T. in large part—well, in part—because he was willing to welcome her sisters over to his house whenever a thunderstorm came up, and also, her sisters had honestly been getting a little bit hard to live with—always snapping at each other it seemed like, not willing to go anywhere unless a storm came up, going on and on about which road did who live on, about who was the cousin of somebody's half-brother. Fussing, and then worried to death about what the other one was thinking, never wanting to be apart but needing to be for some fresh air, it seemed like to Dorothea.

Bea and Mae had always been so nervous about thunder-storms, Mae mostly, and she, Dorothea, always been the one to calm them down, drive them to one of their cousins'. Now Bea and Mae could just come on over to her and Claude T.'s house. Claude T. didn't mind at all.

Claude T. had done other things right during their court-ship—sending her carnations, picking up her medicines at the drugstore, taking her out once a month to Harlan's Steak House even though they served beer and wine. He insisted because of the fine steaks, and she'd gone along with it. He was a good man in his own way. He had his weaknesses, as she reckoned everybody did. His being Cadillacs and a diamond ring were just a little more obvious than normal, but in many ways because these weaknesses didn't directly involve humankind meanness, they weren't the worst kind of weaknesses to have. He didn't drink liquor and make life miserable for everybody around him, like Raleigh Caldwell or Johnny Daniels, but he wadn't afraid of taking medicine either, when he needed it. And he performed in the most ridiculous and funny and awful ways in bed. She'd had to slap his hand, slap, slap, slap, slap, and he'd finally got straight what she wouldn't allow. That Lucinda must have been a regular woman of the night. He'd finally cut all that out and was now a lot more settled down, especially with a little more age on him. And she'd learned one or two things that he *had* to have learned from some book.

47

It had not been easy leaving her sisters. But she'd always been a little more adventurous than either one of them, had taken trips while they'd got more and more fastened to that store and to each other.

They would never know the mountains and valleys of married life. They would always, in an odd sort of way, be married to each other.

One night, twelve years ago, she'd walked into the store and Bea had been sitting in her chair shelling peanuts and Mae had been sitting in hers, knitting. Dorothea was standing there with a smile on her face, thinking that a statement concerning her prospects of marriage might just gently break through whatever it was that had kept her there with them in that store for thirty-two years after their daddy had died, twenty-eight years after their mama had died never knowing her husband was *already* dead, thinking all the while that he was sitting up there outside by the door, dipping snuff, spitting into that same black spot on the ground next to the foundation, believing he was sitting up there talking to anybody who'd come by as if they were the last person on earth, sitting up there still owning the store but retired, happily accepting the work of his three daughters as owed to him for his being their papa, happily accepting their keeping him fed, the store run, and then keeping their mama alive and fed and talked to every day for those four years after he was dead and gone while she believed he was still up there doing all of that. They got to where they would say, "Mama, he was down here a while ago. Remember?" and she'd say, "Oh, yes, yes, now I do. Did he bring me those grapes over there?" and they'd say, "Yes ma'am." It got to be real easy not to tell her he'd died, because that would have put her under for sure, given the weak state she was in. Why not just let her live out her years in a world she believed was there even if it won't.

Dorothea, standing in the dim light that night, thought, had thought for a long time, that the three of them had been holding on to their mama and papa after they were dead in a way that wasn't all good, but was easy—and she was a little afraid of what an announcement of an impending marriage might do. It might gently disturb that whole business of living with what was not there. And when she, fifty-eight years old, said, "What would y'all say if I said I was going to get married?" Bea looked up and said, "I'd say you were going against mama and papa." Mae had then looked up and said, "I think we need to stick together. Did he ask you to marry him?"

"Yes, he did. And I said I wanted to speak to y'all first."

"Well," said Bea, "it looks like you've spoke to us. We do need to stick together though, it seems like to me. We've stuck together this long."

49

"I could still help out around here."

"I don't know why you'd want to do that with a husband to look after."

"It's not like I'm leaving you-all."

"Well, I'd like to know what it is then. You sure can't marry him and bring him here."

Dorothea had sat down in the cane-bottom chair close to the stove and stared straight ahead and had not said one word, feeling like the whole store was shrinking, shrinking, shrinking around her like stretched wet leather, drying, and so she'd just gone downstairs, crawled into her bed, and cried and cried, and both sisters refused to make one move in her direction. Neither one of the three ever mentioned it again. She went ahead and got married anyway.

Dear Claude T. had been so sweet and gentle and led the way for her to become Mrs. Claude T. Clark and to get her job as church secretary and live a Christian life that—what with the exception of Claude T.'s Cadillacs and diamond ring—she was quite happy about. And even without anything else on earth, she'd always have Jesus. And of course even with that gulf, that little gulf—that little problem about her marrying—she'd always have her sisters.

She smoothed her hand over the sheet. She felt the very presence of Jesus Christ of Nazareth. The Lord, in His house.

The sheets were so clean and white. The room temperature was just right.

Maybe she needed a bath, she thought. She'd go ahead with her pills. Then she probably ought to at least go wash off in the sink before she went to bed—take a little sink bath. She reached to the bookshelf, got her medicines, opened them, and put the tablets in her paper cup. Then she stood and made her way to the ladies' room, using the nice sturdy cane Mrs. Weams had brought over—four little legs at the bottom. She'd never seen one like that.

Not far away, Linda Nicholson read the Twenty-third Psalm twice. She'd just found out on the phone from her cousin, Edna Poole, that her granddaughter, Carole, unmarried, was pregnant. She knew all her friends would know by tomorrow, and she was glad she'd been through it all before. People were more sympathetic than you'd think they'd be. / Little Eliza Teasley was laughing, and her best friend Beth Carr was looking at the chocolate from the Baby Ruth stuck between her teeth. Beth was thinking how she was going to keep her own mouth closed until she was pretty sure all her Zero bar was cleared away. / From Sybil White's bedroom: "It come out." "Don't you think I know that?" "Well, stick it back in." "I am!" / Twelve-year-old Frances Hillman was talking on the phone to her new boyfriend, Curtis. The silent pause in their conversation had just lasted one minute and twelve seconds, a record, until Curtis finally said, "Well." / Sarah Coleman, looking forward to Christmas, said to her husband, Ben, "It can be drums or a trumpet, but I believe I'd rather it be a trumpet."

In the bathroom she locked the door, took off all her clothes, and carefully draped them on a chair. Here she was, she thought, naked in the sight of the Lord in the Lord's house, fifteen times the size of a normal house — three stories high — and ten times as quiet.

I come to the garden alone,
While the dew is still on the roses . . .

She turned on the hot water faucet, waited for the water to heat up, turned on the cold to balance it out, ran a little pool of water into the sink, wet her hands and wet herself all between her legs, and on up around under her arms, no soap, then lathered the soap in her hands and lathered herself.

> *And the voice I hear, falling on my ear,*
> *The Son of God discloses.*
> *And He walks with me, and He talks with me . . .*

She let water and soap drip between her legs. She'd get that up with a paper towel.

> *And He tells me I am His own;*
> *And the joy we share as we tarry there,*
> *None other has ever known.*

One of the differences between her and her sisters all her life was that she'd never liked to use a washcloth. There's no tool like your hands, somebody said. She just didn't see any sense in it and besides that, a washcloth got to smelling bad if you didn't keep it washed out, which didn't make any sense.

She ran a fresh little pool of water, cupped her hands, filled them with water, and then rinsed between her legs. She looked in the mirror at her hairdo. It was holding up real good. She rinsed under her arms. She'd get Claude T. to bring her razor in.

She wondered if she'd die before she was stuck in the county home with hair growing under her arms.

Back in her office, she hooked the little door hook for privacy that Claude T. put up when it snowed last year. She cut off the light, sat on the white sheets and looked through the window down at the blinker light, way down there, blinking yellow and lonely. She lay down on her back on the clean sheet, her head on her pillow, feeling all clean between her legs and under her arms.

She should have washed her feet, but it was getting hard to get down there. Her toenails were needing cutting. It was about time for her to call Alease to come and do that. Alease was so thoughtful. And sometime before long she was going to have to get her hair washed and set. She pulled the top sheet and the blanket up over her shoulders.

The phone rang. She'd pulled it close by, and could see from the outside floodlight.

It was Claude T.

"Everything is just fine," she said, "except the swelling is still bad and it hurts unless I prop it up . . . No. I'll be just fine. Maybe a towel or two if you think about it sometime tomorrow . . . Yes . . . Yes, there's all that soup in the white pot, and the two pork chops. Yes . . . Yes. I'm lucky to have the house of the Lord, Claude, to rest my head in. I'm very lucky and very blessed . . . Did you sell that land today? . . . Well, you be good now . . . Bye-bye. I love you, too."

One time he lost that ring for a day and got downright melancholy. Found it in a coat pocket and shouted to high heaven.

She closed her eyes and there against the black was the imprint of the window holding the light from the outside floodlight, a white shadow.

The slightest cool breeze moved in through the window. She couldn't remember feeling so happy and at peace since she was stuck in her office during the snowstorm. Then, and now, she had her little two-eyed hot plate for tomorrow's food, the bath had freshened her, the couch was wide enough and comfortable, and now her ankle, propped up, had stopped hurting completely. She had bathed in the presence of the Lord. She sang softly,

> *I come to the garden alone,*
> *While the dew is still on the roses . . .*

"Dear Lord," she prayed aloud, "thank You for this church, for this community, for our county, and state, and the United States, and our North American continent. We pray for the sick and we pray for all babies without mothers. We're also thankful for our earth, our solar system, the Milky Way, every-thing in the universe, and the universe itself. We pray for those in hardship like Alease Toomey with her brother. Help him see the sin of drinking. Be with Alease. Help us to love one another and for all of us in this church to come to Jesus and accept Him as our Lord and Saviour. In Jesus' name, amen."

NEXT DOOR, PREACHER Crenshaw sat in the parsonage study in the soft chair with flat wooden arms, reading a book by the Reverend Billy Graham about the Holy Land.

Crenshaw's wife was having one of her spells. He figured she'd be over it before too long. This one had been going on eight days, and they didn't usually last over a week, although there was that one that lasted three weeks. She would get down in the dumps and be miserable and it would generally mess things up. She'd blame him for things he didn't do. She'd talk nonstop about the bad condition of the world. He figured if they went to the Holy Land she'd get a spell. When she did get a spell, she'd be unpredictable, sometimes going to Belk Leggett to buy a bunch of dresses they couldn't afford. He'd have to sit down with the budget book and show her, make her take them all back except for maybe one, all the while worrying that church members might find out and say some-thing and get something started.

This business, this *other* business of his, about Cheryl Daniels, was a slight little lark that he could easily control. She wasn't but nineteen. What it was deep down was not the kind of problem he was usually up against. A delightful aspect of Cheryl's personality was that she would kid him, make fun of him. Lisa Rollins—with all her good church and community work—had been the same way a little bit, and had kind of brought it out in Cheryl, he reckoned. As long as he'd been in the pulpit, nobody had ever dared do that very much, because being a man of God was such a serious business deserving serious respect. Saving lost souls, bringing lost sheep to Jesus Christ was dead serious business. It involved eternal life in heaven or hell. But here'd been Lisa Rollins, plump and redheaded and a little older than him, and now Cheryl Daniels, a recently saved soul looking up at him like just about every other woman, young or old, looked at him —with admiration and worship—and he tried not to allow worship of himself. He was bound to deflect the worship of himself off into the direction it needed to go, toward God and Jesus, praise God. But here she had been looking up into his face and there had suddenly come into her eyes a sheer lack of fear and awe, and in place of fear and awe a hint of mockery and fun that was even more pronounced than the way Lisa Rollins was. "Preacher Crenshaw," Cheryl would say, "I bet you are a lot of fun when you want to be." How could somebody from her background be so brash and confident and yet because of that very background so fragile and uncertain of things? It was of paramount importance that she had accepted Jesus Christ as her saviour, and he and Lisa had successfully guided her in that direction, and yet there was this whole pulsing part of her that touched him, even burned him, in a way nothing else ever had. That part had to be of the Devil. What he sometimes thought about doing was shameful. What he wanted to do to her, with her, sometimes overpowered his imagination and intruded right in, no matter how hard he fought it.

"Well, Cheryl, I get excited for the Lord," he'd say.

But he'd done nothing to deny or subdue her obvious—mostly discreet—admiration for him. She was so young and so beautiful and the sight of those big full soft cantaloupes just ran all over him in spite of everything he could do to stop it. It just ran all over him like electricity and he thought of course about his wife, more plump than just plump, bad knees and wrists, having trouble getting around sometimes, and down in the dumps, and here this beautiful young angel-devil who had recently given her heart to Jesus was making fun of him. She saw a side of him, he reckoned. He was kind of glad that side was there, he guessed, but that side of him could not be allowed to cause the sinking, the swallowing up, of all of him and his mission for God. Why for heaven's sake, she was hardly more than a child.

MARJORIE CRENSHAW, THE preacher's wife, was sitting at the kitchen table staring at the big clock shaped like a cat's face, the one her sister had sent from Ohio for the children last Christmas. Marjorie was writing checks for August's bills and had just done the telephone bill. She thought about what they were paying the phone company just to hear over the phone the same things she heard everywhere on earth. From Ada Barker: "What a wonderful sermon that was. Does he ever repeat the same sermon?" From Mabel Lewis: "How in the world did you catch a man like that? It's one thing to be a good preacher, but to be so handsome on top of that." From that new Ben Coleman: "Where's Brother Crenshaw? Can you ask him to call me sometime tomorrow? By the way, does he hunt?" From Ruth Harris: "How in the world did you catch a man like that?" From Hannah Grangerford: "Such lovely children. They favor the preacher, don't they? It must be nice to have your husband home all week. Why are you teaching a Sunday school class? You don't need to be doing that, honey. Don't you have all you can handle with those five children? Is Mr. Crenshaw coming? Tell him what a wonderful sermon that was. Do you know what his favorite food is? I just love his loud ties, don't you? We want y'all to come for dinner. What's Mr. Crenshaw's favorite food?"

AS STEPHEN DRIFTED off to sleep, his asthma medicine doing its dreamy job, he heard parts of *Aunt Margaret's Bible Stories* as his mother read to him.

. . . and so Moses was hidden by his mother in the bullrushes on the river because the Egyptian king was going to kill all the little babies of Israel . . . He was in a basket with tar on it to keep the water out and his sister Miriam was standing watch.

Miriam was the kindest girl in the land. She looked a lot like Cheryl and the woman who came to Stephen when he was dying on the battlefield. When the Egyptian princess found Moses, Miriam went and found Moses' mama, who became his nurse.

. . . Sometimes we see clouds take on mysterious shapes; sometimes they are dark; sometimes they are white or pink and golden. This is God's means of drawing the water up from the earth and sea and carrying it about through the air to let it fall in rain and to water the earth and all the plants and streams and ponds for the animals and for all the people.

After God had made the light and the air, water from the clouds ran down and made rivers and lakes in all the valleys, while the dry hills rose up above them . . . Next He made man in His own image so that he could think, speak, pray, and therefore rule over everything that God had made so far. Humans would be His own sons and daughters. So He made a beautiful place for them to live — with fruit trees and flowers and grass and warm, pleasant weather for them to live in. He called it the Garden of Eden.

. . . And the woman was made by God out of a rib from the man's side. They were called Adam and Eve, and they were the first father and mother of everybody born into the world . . . Each man will have one woman made especially for him, and he will find her some happy day in his life, and each woman will find the one man she is made for. And what God has brought together, no man should take apart.

WHISKEY AND MILK

JACK UMSTEAD PARKED at a peach stand just south of Winnsboro, South Carolina. No customers were around. The woman working there looked a little bit old, but not too old.

"Howdy, howdy," he said. "How about I buy two of your very finest peaches. And if you don't mind, I'd like you to pick them out. One for now and one for down the road."

"Well, okay. Here's a nice one and . . . here's a nice one. That'll be a nickel apiece." She sort of threw back her hair. She wasn't wearing a wedding ring.

"Hot ain't it," he said, exchanging a dime for the small bag.

"It sure is. I don't care if it rains again today. It ain't good for business, but I got to go to town."

"Well . . . hell, you probably don't want to do this, but I'll hold down the fort for a little while if you want to go into town. I ain't in no particular hurry. I've done grocery work all my life."

"That's nice of you, but that's all right."

"I don't blame you. I could steal all your peaches."

"It ain't that. I just wouldn't want you to have to do that."

"I tell you what I'll do. You drive my car into town and if I take your peaches you can have my car. It's a new Buick Eight."

"Ha. How do you know I'll come back?"

"I trust you. And I know somebody as nice as you has got somebody in the wings."

" 'In the wings?' "

"Somebody waiting."

"I wish I did. Well, hell, I'll be back in about twenty minutes, a half hour at the longest. You're mighty nice. Everything is marked, and there's the scales. Thanks a lot. What's your name?"

"My name is Delbert Harris and I'm pleased to meet you."

"I'm Emily."

"Don't worry about a thing. Count your money there now."

After she drove away, Umstead decided he'd ask her if

there was a place around to go to a picture show, or a place to listen to some music—see what that led to.

He looked at the construction of the stand and figured that in any case, he'd show her how the whole peach stand could be—with very little trouble—rigged to take down very easily. You just needed one nail per main joint, with a certain few exceptions. He wondered how many peach stands were in South Carolina and of those how many were portable. Probably very few were portable. Unless they were very small. The smaller the peach stand the more likely it would be portable. There was for sure some kind of formula for that ratio but nobody would ever bother to figure it out.

HARVEY AND STEPHEN walked along home from the store. As Harvey saw it before Stephen was born, the chances of anything going wrong without a child were lower than with. If that child did something wrong, then there you'd be. Harvey would have to live with that, live with all that worry and have his daddy and mama and brothers and sisters be ashamed of what had happened. His mama and daddy and brothers and sisters would then have a harder time in the world because of it. And so one way to avoid all that was just to not have any children. But Alease had wanted a child more than anything it seemed like, and so he'd gone along because she wanted one so much. They lost twins, stillborn, and then when it was almost too late, Stephen came along. Now Harvey was glad. He had a son, after all. A son he was proud of, and at every chance, he took Stephen to see his own mama and papa because that made them happy. When Stephen was a baby, Harvey had taken him every single day.

Before they got to the driveway, Harvey saw Alease's brother, Raleigh, sitting on the front porch floor, his back against the wall, his chin on his chest, as if he'd been flung there.

"Let's go in the back door," said Harvey. "I declare." Nobody in *his* family had ever been a drunk. His papa would never have allowed it. His papa being so strong was a main reason they had all turned out to be good people.

In the house, Harvey kept his eyes straight ahead. "Go sit on the couch, son. I'm going to have to tend to Raleigh. You just sit on the couch." The very idea that Alease would have something to say about *his* brother.

ON THE PORCH, Raleigh said, "Harvey?" He was looking at Harvey's belt buckle. "Harvey, how you *doing*?"

"Raleigh, you got to get up and get in the house."

"Where's Alease?"

When Raleigh, just home from the Great War in 1918,

had stood in the homeplace doorway, his sleeve empty, he had seen a look in Alease's face, a look from his sister who'd grown into a woman. And at that moment, standing there in his uniform, in the few seconds her eyes went down to the empty sleeve and back to his face, right then when her eyes came back to his face, he saw and felt the love that, as he thought he was dying in a muddy field, he knew he'd never again see in his mother's face, the love he remembered from his father's eyes, and the love missing from the faces of all the whores he'd had in England and France, the love he felt, even pictured, as he—among the wounded and dead—had tried to stand up and then had to sit back down, bleeding, the love he'd pictured moving away like a person entering a dark room. But the room's door never closed; he had lived, and at home standing in the doorway, he found all that lost love right there in front of him in this person of his sister, in that look on her face, in her eyes.

"She's at circle meeting," said Harvey. "You got to get up and get in the house, Raleigh. You wet your pants."

"I did not. I don't want to get up and get in the house. I want to stay right where I'm at. I'm comfortable. I live here too, you know."

"Here. Take my hand."

"Aw, Harvey."

FROM THE COUCH, Stephen felt the house shake as Raleigh stumbled up onto his feet. With Uncle Raleigh drunk, his parents were now suddenly little bitty—off to the side some-where—looking up at great big Uncle Raleigh's red face, and hollering at him. His mother would holler the most. She would be afraid.

They came through the living room, his daddy behind Uncle Raleigh, holding him up. Then his father called, "Stephen! Come open the bathroom door."

Stephen opened the door, then moved on ahead of them into the small bathroom.

Uncle Raleigh turned so that his back was to Stephen. "I don't want to take a bath," he said. He leaned toward Stephen's daddy, then stepped on his toe. His daddy pushed him back, hard.

Stephen watched his uncle start to fall, above him. He realized that if he didn't jump into the corner, his uncle—this giant tree—would fall on him.

His uncle held to his daddy—they were falling together —then turned loose, reached out and back, grabbed the medicine cabinet and held on as it pulled loose from the wall. "What the damn hell," he said. The medicine cabinet crashed against the back of the commode, exploding the mirror. His uncle hit the floor—his rear end, his shoulders, then his head, hard enough to bounce up, stop, then slowly lower itself, eyelids closing, as Stephen's daddy, first dancing and fighting to stand up, then collapsed on top of him.

The medicine cabinet hit the floor, scattering bottles and tubes.

His daddy raised up on one elbow, looked at his uncle's face, at Stephen. "Go get the broom, son. I'm afraid to move. There's glass all——"

"I can't get out."

"Just . . . just step over us somehow. Be careful of the glass."

"That was like a bum' went off," said Stephen. He got over them, slowly, carefully, and in the kitchen he met Mrs. Odum. She had a bag of clothespins hung around her neck and some white underwear in her hand.

"I HEARD A crash," said June Odum. "Is everything all right?"

"Daddy fell on Uncle Raleigh."

"They fighting?"

"No ma'am. Uncle Raleigh had to go to the bathroom. I got to go sweep up the mirror. The mirror broke."

"That's seven years bad luck. Here. Here's the broom. No, I'll do it. Let me just put down these underwear some-where. I *would* have that one with the waistband loose."

Mrs. Odum saw the soles of four shoes—two facing up, two facing down—and beyond that two men entangled. The one on top moved and several slivers of glass fell to the floor.

"Harvey, is that you?"

"Yes. Can you get a broom, June?"

"I got one right here. What in the world was y'all doing?"

"I was bringing Raleigh to the bathroom."

"Don't look like he quite made it, you know, all the way. Lord, there's glass everywhere."

"Can you . . . just sweep it from around us?"

"I don't . . . I don't think I can get in here. This is the littlest bathroom. Course there ain't no reason to have a great *big* bathroom, I always said."

"Daddy," said Little Steve, "I'm getting asthma."

"Take a pill and lay down on the couch. I can't help you right this minute, son."

"But there's reason enough to have a big *closet,* I always said. Course if I had a choice, I'd have a big bathroom *and* a big closet."

"The pills were in the medicine cabinet, Daddy," said Little Steve.

"I don't think they're in there now," said June. "But if you could have two bathrooms then it wouldn't be as much need for either one to be so big—especially if there was just one person using each one."

"They're in a medicine bottle somewhere," said Little Steve, looking around.

Raleigh opened his eyes.

"You'd just need one towel rack, for example," said June. "Hey there, Raleigh. What kind of bottle?" she asked Little Steve.

"Early Times," said Raleigh. "All things equal."

"I don't know," Little Steve was saying. "My mama just gives them to me."

"Where the . . . ," said Raleigh, "the . . . where the god-dang are we?"

"You're in the bathroom floor it looks like to me," said June. "And there ain't a whole lot of room for you to maneuver."

Harvey slowly raised to one knee, then stood up. "You've got to get up, Raleigh, so I can see if you're cut. I cut my hand."

"Can I see?" said Little Steve.

"I think I'll just lay here for a minute," said Raleigh, "until this lady brings me a bottle."

"It's June, Raleigh. June Odum. I don't have a bottle—that kind. Raleigh, you know how much we all hate to see you in such a fix as this. There's not a nicer man in Listre than you when you're sober. And I don't have no bottle for you. Or for anybody else. It's against all I stand for."

"We've got to get you up, Raleigh," said Harvey. "Stephen, are those your pills in the corner there?"

"I think, maybe."

"Pick them up."

"Harvey," Raleigh said, "I think . . . . where'd she say we was at?"

"We're in the *bath*room. Let me see the broom, June."

June watched Harvey sweep glass from around Raleigh and into a corner. "Go take a pill, son," said Harvey, "and lay down, and I'll be in there in a minute. I don't think you're cut, Raleigh."

"That boy shouldn't be taking pills," said Raleigh.

STEPHEN HELD A pill in his hand. His baby bottle of sweet milk and Karo syrup stood in the refrigerator, waiting. He reached in and got it. It was cold and wet. His mama had some way of heating it on the stove. He placed a pill in his mouth, then the baby bottle nipple, drank, and swallowed the pill.

"Let me help you," said Mrs. Odum. "That old asthma just gets in your chest, don't it, son?"

"Yes ma'am. I have to drink milk out of a bottle. If I drink out of a glass, it makes me vomit."

"Yes, I know. You come on in here and I'll tuck you in the couch so you can get you some rest. Some things in this old world we just can't help, can we?"

"No ma'am."

"Your uncle is not setting a very good example."

Mrs. Odum placed a blanket over Stephen, tucked it in. "Do you want me to read you a story?"

"Yes ma'am."

She picked up *Aunt Margaret's Bible Stories* from the coffee table. "Do you have a favorite story?"

"Little Moses getting hid in the water, or Joseph and his coat and his brothers."

"Let's see," said Mrs. Odum. "See what I can find."

For Stephen, this was a good, but sometimes a little bit scary, part of the day: when he heard one of Aunt Margaret's Bible stories and sometimes a story out of the Bible itself—over there on the coffee table, too. Things happened in the Bible a long time ago when the Bible was a place and a time together. The Bible was the main real place and the main real time. They had camels and donkeys. And God would just all of a sudden strike a bad person dead. He turned a woman into a salt lick because she looked back at a city. And Stephen got stoned to death: people throwing rocks—great big rocks—at him, until he died because big rocks were piled up all over him. That was as bad as being sent to the electric chair. And there were the good things like when the dove came to Noah with a twig in its mouth and Noah knew the flood was over. Everybody on the ark was going to be saved.

"Now," said Mrs. Odum, "let's get comfortable. Put your head in my lap if you want to, and I'll read and show you the pictures. Let's do this one.

When little Isaac was born, Abraham was overjoyed and loved him dearly.

But then God called Abraham to do a strange and terrible thing. He was to take his dear son Isaac to the top of a hill, and there to kill him and offer him up to God as a sacrifice, as if he had been a calf or a lamb.

God was the man way up there in the sky with the white beard who looked down and said to do this. A sacrifice meant cut his head off, just kill him because God said so, which Abraham was going to do and Isaac didn't know what was going to happen.

But just as Abraham had the knife ready to slay his son, God called out of Heaven: "Lay not thine hand upon the lad, neither do thou anything unto him: for now I know that thou lovest Me, seeing thou hast not withheld thine only son."

That was it. It was just a trick that made Abraham sad at first, and it scared Isaac because he thought he was going to get killed with the knife right at the last minute because his daddy had been hiding it from him. That's exactly the time that Abraham was pulling out that hid knife.

As Abraham loved Isaac, he loved God more, and we must all be willing to give up anything God wants us to; but you see God only did this to test Abraham's faith, and He would not let him do a wrong thing. God will not make us give up anything we ought to have.

"Now," said Mrs. Odum, "you want me to ask you these questions?"

"My mama don't."

"Well, let's just try a few. Now. What was Abraham's son's name?"

"Isaac."

"Good. And what did God tell Abraham to do?"

"Cut Isaac's head off."

"Well, I don't know about that. He was just going to make him a sacrifice, which is . . . do you know what a sacrifice is?"

"When you cut somebody's head off?"

"Well, no, it's more like when you give something up . . . like a piece of pie. Like when you give up a piece of pie. You sacrifice it. You just give something up. Abraham was going to give up Isaac, see."

"He was going to cut his head off."

"No, I don't think he was going to do that. He was just going to, ah . . . I've always thought it was some kind of burning. Let's see if we can find another story. Just a little short one. How about . . . let's see, here's one that's just a little over a page. It's called 'Seven Hundred Years of Jewish History.' Oh, and look at this picture—Jacob and the angel. Look at that. Now that's right before they had a wrestling match. Did you know about that?"

"No ma'am. I can't remember."

"Now, that was real interesting. This angel kept Jacob up all night wrestling and finally it was almost a draw until Jacob found a secret place in the angel's back. Here, put your head back down. I believe you're getting sleepy. Your mama will be home in just a little bit, I'll bet. You go on to sleep, now."

WHEN ALEASE CAME home, in through the back door, she thought she smelled Raleigh, but she didn't want to believe that. In the living room, she touched Stephen's bottle and asked Harvey, "Why didn't you warm his bottle?"

Harvey, broom in hand, just looked at her.

"Is Raleigh here?" she asked.

"Yes. He's drunk. And he made a big mess in the bathroom. Pulled down the medicine cabinet."

In Raleigh's bedroom, Alease sat on her brother's bed. "Raleigh, look at you. Why do you do this? Why?"

"I haven't done nothing, Alease."

"We've got to change your pants."

"I need a little drink."

"Have you got a bottle?"

"In my pocket. I think. June was 'pose to get me a new one."

"Sit up. I'll swanee. Raleigh, you *know* better than this." Coming in here like this. Why did he *do* this?

"Don't be mad at me, Alease. You know I love you. You know I always have."

STEPHEN LISTENED FROM the couch in the next room. He heard his mother getting ready, getting ready to really holler at Uncle Raleigh. One time somebody had been there, two or three aunts and uncles for some reason, and his uncle Raleigh had come home drunk, and they got him in the living room and he started talking about something, about something funny. He was telling a story, and they all laughed and laughed, and then when the others went home, his mother had lit into Uncle Raleigh and Uncle Raleigh had ended up crying and blubbering, and the whole time all of this went on, Stephen remembered, he'd been on the couch drinking warm milk and Karo syrup from his bottle.

ALEASE WATCHED AS Raleigh reached to his back pants pocket. "I got a little old pint right there, I do believe." She watched him slowly pull it out, hold it up, look at it. "I just need one little drink to get me through."

"If you get up and take a bath, Raleigh—you smell terrible—I'll give you a little drink."

She got Raleigh's shirt off, his undershirt, shoes and socks, finally his wet trousers, and led him in his boxer shorts to the bathroom, where she got him seated on the covered commode. She looked around, noticed a shard of glass in the tub. She lifted it out. The medicine cabinet was leaning against the wall. It was just like Harvey not to put it back up where it belonged. And he should have seen that piece of glass. She rinsed out the tub, then put the stopper in the tub drain and drew warm water. Raleigh would lie out somewhere and die if she didn't do this. There was nobody else willing. Harvey wouldn't do it. Raleigh had nobody but her. He had a good mind and heart. She hated for Stephen to see this, but there was nothing else to do. She could explain it to him as he got a little older—the awfulness of it all, what all Raleigh had had to go through. Stephen could learn from it. Learn to never touch alcohol.

Raleigh, dressed in clean, dry clothes, sat at the kitchen table while Alease did, at this stage, all she knew to do: pour him a drink, a little drink. Wean him off it.

"Aw, Alease, that ain't enough."

"Raleigh, that's all you're getting and then it's time for you to go to bed."

"Go to bed?"

"Yes. I'll lay down with you, if you'll go to sleep."

STEPHEN HEARD THEM talking from the couch where he lay very still except for his lips moving on the bottle nipple. His eyes, with heavy lids, fluttered. He imagined that the cold milk and Karo syrup mixture was warm. The little yellow pill had cleared his chest and made him sleepy and now would bring strange dreams.

His mama and his uncle were going to take a nap together. His mother was the one in the world to take care of Uncle Raleigh.

NEXT MORNING JUNE Odum stood in the open back door at the Toomey house. "Alease?" she called. "*Alease?*"

Alease heard her from the living room, answered, went to the kitchen.

"I see Raleigh's been drinking again," said June. "Anything I can do?"

"Not that I can think of. Come on in and sit down. I was

just cleaning up a little bit. He's still asleep." She stood the broom against the pantry door, wondered what time he might get up. "Harvey's got Stephen down at the blinker light."

"Well, I'm just sorry about it and I know it just worries you to death."

"It sure does, June."

"There's no nicer man in the world when he's sober than Raleigh Caldwell."

"I know it."

"No neater man."

"That's right."

"I was in the yard and heard him and Harvey fall in the bathroom. Did y'all get your medicine cabinet back up?"

"Not yet. I got all the glass up out of the floor, though."

Alease found an ashtray for June, then sat down with her at the kitchen table. She thought about the work she had to do, but this was all right for a few minutes.

"Did Stephen get over his asthma?" asked June.

"He did. Those pills usually help out."

"What is it you reckon makes him vomit when he drinks milk outen a glass?"

"I don't know. He's ashamed of it. Hides his bottle. I've never heard of such a thing, and Dr. Fountain said just go ahead and feed him a bottle and he'll outgrow it."

"Sometimes I wish I'd used a bottle when Fred was a baby.

He chewed on my titties something fierce. They never *did* toughen up. I think it was some kind of condition he had. I never heard of such. His gums were as hard as rocks. It was like he had rock gums."

"I don't know what I'd done without a bottle once Stephen started vomiting."

June took a draw off her Pall Mall. Silence. She looked at the yellow daisies in a jar on the windowsill, turned her head and blew smoke. "You just can't beat yellow for a color, can you?"

Alease was glad to have the back door open to the morning, and to have June over to talk for a little while, but it was time to get back to work. She hoped Raleigh would sleep long enough and June would leave in time for her to hear "Break the Bank" on the radio while she did her ironing. She'd have to explain some more to Stephen about how what Raleigh did was a sin but not bad enough for the electric chair. She'd have to fix dinner. She'd fix ham sandwiches. That ham was only about half gone—plenty more. She'd have to keep weaning Raleigh. She'd have to be real firm with him. She'd have to sweep the front porch and keep Raleigh off it until he got sober. She'd have to put away the breakfast dishes, call Harvey on their new telephone, and tell him to bring home a fresh chicken and some string beans. It had gotten to be too much going next door to borrow June's phone. She might fix some pinto beans. June had gotten the idea from somewhere of putting a cut-up cabbage core in her pinto beans. Alease wished she could have told that to her mother because they had always thrown the cabbage core away. She wished Stephen could have gotten to know her mother. June's pintos were good cooked that way, and with a whole onion dropped in there. Alease didn't hardly ever think of food but what she didn't think of her mother.

⁓

THAT AFTERNOON, PREACHER Crenshaw drove past Train's Place on the way to visit Alease Toomey about the recent trouble with her brother.

Somehow beer-drinking out of doors at Train's had bled into the community so slowly it had escaped public condemnation. The fact of apparent abstinence at the flintrock, the grocery, the Blaine sisters', the barbershop, and up at the grill helped keep the blinker light intersection wholesome enough. And besides, Train's was just a little too close to home for direct lambasting. Though Lord knows, drinking *was* lambasted from his pulpit. But just about anybody who drank beer at Train's Place had relatives in the church and there was no need to go stirring up trouble close to home. Unless it got worse.

Alease Toomey's house looked neat and trouble-free from

the outside. It was white with a nice lawn and flowers all around. He needed to be with her for a prayer at least. She was not one to call on him or come for a visit. She was an independent sort. But Mrs. Odum said she was in need and Raleigh Caldwell had always been a bad problem when he was drunk. An embarrassment. And while he, Crenshaw, was there he might mention to Mrs. Toomey his own problem with his secretary, Mrs. Clark. She'd up and moved into her office. She was *living* there. Mrs. Toomey was discreet, for sure. He'd never heard of her telling anybody one single thing. He needed to maybe see what Mrs. Toomey thought about the Mrs. Clark situation.

STEPHEN WAS SITTING in the dirt at the garage entrance, rolling his little metal trucks through their chores of hauling important dirt along their new roads, completing important jobs. Each truck was solid in a way Stephen adored. He saw the preacher's green Ford, didn't recognize it. Then he recognized the preacher when he got out of his car. Why was he coming over there?

Mr. Crenshaw came up, said a word or two, then went to the back door and knocked. Mr. Crenshaw was the king of the church, and the church was the king building of the whole country around there. Stephen had seen Mr. Crenshaw up on the stage behind the wood thing, he'd seen Mr. Crenshaw walk back and forth up there and raise his hand toward heaven and holler until he got red in the face, hollering about what hell was like and what heaven was like and telling them to hurry up and accept Jesus as their saviour because when Jesus came back you'd better be saved.

Since his uncle Raleigh and his mama and Preacher Crenshaw were all in the house, he decided he would go in and see what was happening.

His mama and the preacher were sitting at the kitchen table. The preacher was praying:

". . . and for the afflictions and the hardships brought by alcohol we pray for release. We ask Thy guidance in conquering the evil of the material excesses we experience every day. Help us, oh Lord, to fight temptation in all its disguises. Help us to be true, and clean, and pure, in Jesus' blessed name. Amen."

"Stephen, honey, you go on back outside and play while me and Mr. Crenshaw talk a little while."

"He's growing up into a fine young man. Stephen, what do you want to be when you grow up, son?"

"A fireman."

"Well that's good—and you know you can be a good Christian fireman. There's nothing wrong with that."

"He's also thinking about being a missionary," said Mrs. Toomey. "He's almost seven. Honey, you run on back outside."

His uncle Raleigh stood in the kitchen door. "Hello, Mr. Caldwell."

The preacher stood, shook his uncle's hand.

"Go on outside, son," said his mother.

Stephen wanted to see what happened with all those big parts of the world there together in one room, but his mother escorted him out the back door, and he returned to his spot in front of the garage where his trucks waited for their jobs of driving in straight lines, and curves, and turning over.

HARDER THAN A diamond, longer than a longitude, deeper than all space, Raleigh wanted heat in his throat and stomach and then the magic of it spreading up to his head, releasing him to love the world—and be loved—and to hold on. He didn't want no goddamned son of a bitching preacher in the kitchen. "What are you doing here?"

"I come to spend just a little time with Alease. Frankly, her having to deal with your drinking, Raleigh, can be kind of hard on her, as you probably know."

"She's my sister and what she's dealing with is none of your business." Who in the tarnation did he think he was?

"We'd have to ask her about that, I suppose."

"I don't think we have to ask her nothing. She promised me a little drink."

"Raleigh, I'm not going to give you a little drink, yet. Preacher Crenshaw, sometimes I have to wean him off his whiskey."

Raleigh stepped forward. "Wean bean Dizzy Dean. I need a little drink to get me going and then I'll get out there and cut that grass." There were things a man could do around the house. Where was Harvey Parvey?

"Raleigh, you're not in any shape to cut grass. Preacher Crenshaw, I'll walk you out to your car. I appreciate you coming by."

"That's okay, Alease. I need to be getting on up to the hospital."

"To the hospital?" says Raleigh. "You mean you got to go to work today?"

"Raleigh, you go in the living room right now and I'll tend to you in a minute."

"That's exactly where I was headed. That's exactly where I was headed."

PART 2

The Man in the Buick Eight

A SPITNEW FACE

AS HE PULLED in, Jack Umstead noted the name
"Redding" on the big sign——REDDING BRO. GULF SERVICE
STATION, TRAIN REDDING, PROPRIETOR——hanging from
an inverted L-shaped pole. Dripping water sparkled in sunlight against a dark sky on down the road. Beyond the intersection was a rock-walled store, lighted by the sun, general
store it looked like, whole thing made out of big rocks.
Across the road a grocery store——boy sitting on the porch
step.

He got out, shut the door——a solid clunk. With this car
he felt plum rich. He looked around. Tacked on to the grocery store was what looked like had to be a feed room.
Beyond that, another store, maybe a store and house combination, then another——PENDERGRASS AUTO SHOP AND GRILL.

A barbershop across the road.

Whole place looked settled, ripe, timid, kind of stupid. Just right.

"What can I do for you?"

"Fill her up. Check the oil." He leaned against his Buick. This service station man's eyes were a little closer together than they ought to be and he didn't have a lot of chin. Looked like a talker. "You're one of the Reddings, ain't you?"

"That's right. I'm Blake."

Umstead waited the appropriate time. "I got some relatives over on the other side of Traveler's Rest." He spit from between his tongue and upper teeth. Looked around. "Just getting back to see them."

"Yeah?"

The pump dinged on each dollar. It took a while.

"Except I don't think I remember that blinking light," said Umstead. "How long's that been there?"

"Oh, about eight years. Nine. Since the mule-truck head-on—right after that."

"Mule-truck head-on. Now I do remember hearing something about that. I'm trying to remember whose mule that was."

"My brother was driving the truck. Train."

"Train Redding. That's right. I do remember that."

"It was Butch Gaylord's mule." Blake pulled the nozzle from the gas tank. "Who's your family?"

"Jones. Joneses. But somehow we ain't no kin to the Joneses right around here. We moved to South Carolina, then Mississippi when we left here. I try to come back when I can. The place hadn't changed all that much really. I'm on the way south from Richmond where I been visiting a army buddy."

"That'll be two sixty-five on the gas." Blake checked the oil. "Oil looks good. This is a nice car." He slammed the hood.

"Yeah, I got a pretty good deal on it. Traded a forty-nine Ford."

"Buick's a good automobile."

STEPHEN LOOKED TOWARD the slamming hood. The new man leaning up against the big black car talking to Mr. Blake looked skinny but strong at the same time. He was wearing some kind of boots, and dungarees, and a yellow shirt. He wore wire glasses and his hair was black and kind of curly in a way that made Stephen believe that the man was probably a happy beer drinker.

INSIDE TRAIN'S PLACE, Blake made change.

Umstead asked, "How old's that dog out there?"

"Sixteen."

"Damn."

"So you just visiting, huh?"

"Yeah. I'll be around for a few days, maybe a week, visit some of my folks and then head on back to Mississippi. What's that dog's name?"

"Trouble."

"He's full-blooded, ain't he?"

"Yep. English style, with them bowlegs. And he can tell the weather. Depends on where he takes his morning nap. There you go, two dollars and thirty-five cents."

"Who's he belong to?"

"Train."

Umstead looked around. "All things equal, I guess if I had to be in a pasture with a bull I'd rather him have a dog hanging on his nose."

"Where you from in Mississippi?"

"Clarksdale."

"I had a cousin had a grandma in Corinth."

"Don't know nobody in Corinth."

It was kind of dark in there. Candy counter, hoop of cheese, few canned goods, junk. Naked woman calendar. Ummmm. Somebody in a wheelchair behind the candy counter near a table of . . . radios? Had to be the owner. Certain mental nerves magically told you things like that.

"How you doing?" Umstead said.

"All right."

"You're Train, ain't you?"

"That's right."

"You probably don't remember me. I lived over the other side of Traveler's Rest for a few years with some kinfolks and I spent some time around these parts, worked some in Summerlin."

"Yeah, well . . . You any kin to Marcus Jones?"

"Who was his daddy?"

"Sam."

"No, not close kin, not a Sam that I recall."

Umstead bought a slice of hoop cheese to go, took another look at the calendar—"I keep forgetting what day it is," he said—paid his respects, went out and sat in the car for a minute, checked his rearview mirror. Little boy across the road sitting on the steps. Smoking? Little boy smoking? Now there was a good source.

"YOU NOTICE WHAT he called T.R.?" said Train to Blake.

"Called it Traveler's Rest."

"First time I heard that in a long time."

"I think people used to call it that sometime back, didn't they?"

"Not that I know of."

Albert Copeland sat on the Weams's pond bank with his sons, Thatcher and Meredith. He was talking to Meredith. "You take the head and just push it in like that and kind of just go ahead and turn the whole thing wrongsideoutwards, see, and it's all juicy yellow, and the fish like that. So then you just hook it. See?" / Linda Clovis, over in T.R., was hemming her grandfather's coat. He'd had a stroke and his left side drooped now and she was hemming the coat on an angle so it would hang level all the way around.

THE STRANGER WALKED into the grocery store, came back out with a Pepsi-Cola and a bag of peanuts, and sat on the bench. "I thought them was real cigarettes you was smoking," he said.

Stephen shook his head.

"What's your name?"

"Stephen."

"Stephen what?"

"Stephen Toomey."

"You know where all the cigarette smoke in the world goes?"

"No sir."

"Makes white clouds." He tossed peanuts into his mouth one at a time. "You know where all the rubber offen tires goes?"

Stephen shook his head.

"Makes black clouds. Know where farts go?"

Stephen looked at the man.

"A fart, poot, you know—*pbrruuuet*. Ain't you ever farted? Pooted? You call it a poot?"

"Ye . . . yessir." He was talking ugly.

"Well, you know where they go to?"

"No sir."

"They go in your ears, come out your nose, get in your socks and hide 'tween your toes."

Stephen thought: This man is a beer drinker up close.

"You ever had anybody find a penny behind your ear?"

"Yessir. Mr. Ferrell did."

The man stood, walked over. When he got close Stephen could smell him, a smell like fresh, clean fish. He pulled a penny from behind Stephen's ear and handed it to him. "I guess this is yours, Budrow."

Stephen looked at the penny, at Abraham Lincoln. He felt behind his ear.

"This is a right nice store," said the man. "Who runs it?"

"Uncle Steve. And my daddy."

"I see." The man chewed a peanut. "Well, it sure is a nice store." He sat back down on the bench. "I think it's a little nicer than the one next door. Who runs that?"

"The Blaine sisters."

"I see."

"They drive to Mrs. Clark's house when it lightnings."

"They drive off when it lightnings, huh?"

"Yessir."

"Well, well. Then they gone now?"

"Yessir."

"I see. How you know all this?"

"My mama cuts their toenails." He saw Miss Bea's long second toes. She'd tell him that that meant she was supposed to be rich, and then she'd laugh.

"Okay."

"They got a pen of chickens down in the gully. And they got fifteen cats. They shoot their chickens with a four-ten."

"You sure it's fifteen?"

"Yessir."

"Shoot their *chickens?*"

"Yessir."

"Well, I remember these two old ladies where I grew up. They ran a store just like that one and they sold little naked chickens that they'd hacked and picked, and every Saturday night they'd go swimming in a pond down behind their store and they'd take off them old black dresses and their ribs showed up green in the moonlight that shined down through them old black trees and they'd jump in the water and swim around naked before the mosquitoes ate them up. What you think about that?"

"Not but one of the Blaine sisters is skinny."

"Okay." The man stood, stuck his empty Pepsi bottle in the drink carton. "You keep your nose clean," he said.

HE DROVE TO the Settle Inn, a place he'd noticed a little ways back. The eight small one-room cabins resembled the main building—steep, A-frame roofs, with wide overhangs. Swiss-like. This was going to work out just fine.

The man, a Bert Sessoms, gave him a flyswatter and a key to cabin 6. He liked this place: Listre. He'd settle on Plan A as the old women's store. He didn't much think he'd find anything better, but he'd learned not to rush.

On the way back down to Train's Place, he noticed that the flintrock store across the intersection looked yellow-white in the late-afternoon sun. Behind it the sky was still dark with the storm somewhere up the road to the east.

At Train's he sat on the outside bench under the drive-under and nursed a Blatz. The bench was backed against the brick wall. Trouble was asleep on a doormat in a cardboard box. Two slender iron pillars supported the drive-under roof, and just to the inside of each stood a Gulf gas pump. The floor to the drive-under was concrete and inclined up to the road on his left and down to the road on his right. Around to the side was a pit for engine work.

Up across the intersection, an old woman and a man came out of the door of the Blaine sisters' store. So the sisters were back. She opened the lid to some kind of long box. She was holding . . . an ice pick? Yes. She chipped, then pulled a page of newspaper from under her arm and wrapped up what looked like a nickel block of ice, and handed it to the customer. She was dressed in black and reminded Umstead of his Aunt Prissy. He could still smell her snuff and woodsmoke smell. Another old woman came out, not skinny. Sweeping. Sweeping water. *She* was dressed in black. There was a garage next to their store, a clothesline with two white sheets on it—they sure enough lived in there, down in the back. There shouldn't be any resistance to speak of, no iron bars. They for sure had a stash in there somewhere, under something, in something. He saw himself kicking in the back door during a rainstorm, saw himself down in there with them cats all around, going through stuff, throwing stuff out on the floor until he found the stash and then hit the road for points north.

A man over at the barbershop backed out of the door, reached onto the inside wall, and cut off the revolving barber pole, closed the door and locked it, a screen door against his back all the while. A possibility, but he probably took his money home.

A bell rung on the Blaine sisters' screen door as Umstead entered. Inside was darker than inside the gas station and had a lived-in feel, a musty smell. Cats. A couple of big stuffed house chairs were in there, three cats he could see to count— damn, one with three legs, not even a stump.

"Come here, kitty . . . Well, get under the table then."

"Can I help you?" It was the skinny one. She'd come up the stairs. She did not seem friendly.

"You sell licorice?"

"Sure do."

"I need three or four sticks. It's getting hard to find."

"Well, we got some." She opened the sliding candy counter door.

"How you stay in business with all these other stores around?"

"We sell licorice, for one thing." She handed him the brown paper bag. "That'll be eight cents. Plus we don't do a lot of fancy stuff. Ice and chickens, mostly."

"How long you-all been here?"

"My daddy opened this store in 1909 and it's been open since."

Umstead paid. "Save on electricity, too, don't you."

"What's that?"

"It's good to have electricity, ain't it."

"It's gone run us outen the ice business. More and more Frigidaires."

"Yeah, you're right about that. I used to live over the other side of Traveler's Rest, years ago. My cousin—"

"T.R."

"What?"

"I said, 'T.R.' We call it T.R. around here."

"Oh, yes ma'am. T.R. My cousin wrote me a letter about Train and the mule head-on."

She came out from behind the counter and started for the door.

"I said my cousin wrote—"

"I got to close now if you don't want nothing else. Come back again sometime. Is that a real mustache?"

"Yes ma'am, it is. It's my cookie duster."

"You don't say. I never liked hair on a man's face."

"Better'n hair on a woman's face."

"What's that?"

"I said I used to work for a man that shaved his whole head."

"That ain't what you said."

"What?"

"Never mind."

BEA BLAINE WATCHED through the door window as smarty-pants drove away. She watched to see which way he turned at the blinker light. He turned right. She moved to the side window and watched across the back field as he drove on west—but he turned in at the Settle Inn, parked, got out of his car, got something out of the backseat, and went into a cabin.

Downstairs, she sat down in her rocking chair near Mae, who was still listening to "The Farm Report," about halfway through now. "There's a man staying at the Settle Inn that's got one of them pencil-thin mustaches," she said.

"How you know he's staying at the Settle Inn?" asked Mae. Her face was big and soft. She was knitting.

"I saw him drive in there. I thought you were going to say how'd I know he had a mustache?"

"You could see his mustache all that far?"

"No. He was upstairs—I just sold him some licorice and then I watched him drive on down to the Settle Inn. He was a smarty-pants."

"What'd he want?"

"I saw his mustache while he was in the store. Some licorice. He's got folks in T.R. he says. But he's too good to stay with them."

"I don't know what anybody'd want to eat that stuff for."

"Because they like it."

"Well, I know that. But I'm saying I don't know *why* they'd like it."

"Same as they like anything else," said Bea. "They just like the taste of it."

"I got so vinegar gives me bad dreams. Awful dreams. I had one last night where I couldn't get home. *No*body would talk to me. Big crowd. Women, men milling around. Couldn't find my handbag. I asked and asked and nobody would help. I went in a bathroom and turned on a big *radio* in there and that's when I woke up and had the hardest time going back to sleep. I kept tasting that vinegar."

"Stop eating it."

"I am," said Mae.

"Nobody helps nobody no more. We need some help around here."

"Well, look at Claude T.," said Bea. "He's not no more interested in this store than nothing. I don't know of a man that I ever knew that would have been interested in it. Staying in one place all this time."

"Papa."

"Besides Papa."

"That little Toomey boy seems nice to me," said Mae. "He's got good manners. His mama's seen to that. And he's old enough to do some errands. We could pay him a little something to do some things—some bending-over things, cleaning-up things."

"Shoot the chickens," said Bea. "I told his daddy he could be our chicken shooter. He's plenty old enough. That little four-ten don't kick to amount to nothing."

OUTSIDE THE SETTLE Inn, Umstead unloaded his leather bag, his film projector, and his paper bags of film reels. Next to the road were two chairs and a picnic table, a place he could sit and watch cars pass.

Inside: a double bed with a blue spread under a folded-up army blanket, two cane-bottomed chairs, a table with water pitcher, glass, big bowl, bar of soap, towel, and washcloth, lamp, a hanging picture of some flowers, and a pot under the bed.

He took off his pants, laid them across a chair, poured water into the bowl, placed a bar of soap in the water, took off his shirt, and carefully sank it in the water. Normally, while that shirt soaked for a day, he wore his other yellow one, or his only other everyday shirt——a blue and black plaid flannel. He had two pairs of blue jeans, folded, a navy blue pin-striped business suit on a hanger, a pressed white dress shirt in a box, three neckties, and a week's worth of underwear.

He took off his glasses, socks, underwear, lay down on the bed, naked, put his hands behind his head, and went to sleep.

When he woke up ten minutes later, he ate his cheese, drank some water straight out of the pitcher, set up his sixteen-millimeter projector, threaded one of his movies and watched it on the wall. It was the one about the farmer's daughter on the hay in the barn when the field hand comes in.

The films kept him out of trouble with women. He could always make up things in his head but, hell, these films were almost as good as the real thing. Same ones over and over. Would the time ever come, he wondered, when not only could you see it happen, it could really happen with some kind of rubberized electronic woman——happen without you being involved with a actual person, with a personality that would get in the way of everything? Sometimes he thought about retiring and going into that kind of business. Making rubber women. He figured he could plan it all out if he had a partner who could build some kind of tiny motor that would make it go hump, hump, hump.

He decided to drive around, do his research, see if there were any more stores that looked better than the old ladies'. He drove east toward the intersection, looked at the stores again, thought about how he could always fall back on selling. Selling anything. Hell, if he had to he could sell God. Plenty of people did.

The afternoon sun was lighting up tree bark like it was on fire. He thought about the time he was on that island off the Texas coast and watched the sun set over the water, his shadow getting longer and longer on the sand down the beach along the surf. When the sun touched the flat horizon, he realized his shadow went not just down along the beach, but on out into space as far as the light of the sun would ever reach. He waved his hand and figured that that shadow with the waving hand would be riding a light wave on out into space and on and on as far away as the stars and then some. That seemed like something some kind of prehistoric tribe might have thought about. When the sun was up above, your shadow didn't go nowhere hardly.

Yep, he felt pretty comfortable around this little blinker-light community. About as risk-free as you could ask for. He drove past a church, big church. Later on, he would see if a door was open.

A school was across from the church. He turned in: a ball field and grandstand behind the school, a grandstand like he'd grown up with—with a roof. He'd never seen another grandstand so much like the one in Rolling Fork. How about that? "Home sweet home," he said out loud to himself.

Up a little hill behind the grandstand was a . . . an old one-room school? No, by golly, that was a little church. There was the cross. A little boarded-up church. They'd closed it down and maybe built the big brick one across the road. Or this one had got elbowed out of use. The one he'd gone to in Mississippi was like this one, except wider and a little heftier and had two bell towers in front, and two front doors. He'd climbed up in there with the bell one time when his sister had run away and he'd looked out to see if he could see her. He'd thought God would help him—help him see for a long, long way, see her walking down some road the way she always walked along some road ten steps or so in front of him swinging her arms, and he'd be able to holler out to her. But once he climbed up in there and looked out, he hadn't been able to see anywhere hardly.

He drove back out to the highway. A sign stood on the front lawn at the school:

PICTURE SHOW AND POPCORN
EVERY FRIDAY NIGHT. 7:30. 25 CENTS TOTAL

Mr. Weams, in his house behind the church, sitting in the chair beside the couch, called to Mrs. Weams to come help him. His toe was hung in his sock opening. That was the second time that had happened lately. He couldn't bend far enough forward to get it loose, and if he dropped the sock on the floor he wouldn't be able to reach it. Mrs. Weams came from the kitchen and helped him. She'd been peeling potatoes. / At the Pendergrass Grill, Cheryl set a cup of coffee in front of a customer. / Over at Listre Grocery, Big Steve and Harvey slid the heavy wood-slat vegetable baskets off the porch and into the store. / In his backyard, Charles Latham told his bird dog Buck to sit. The dog sat, and Charles rubbed him under the neck, scratched with his fingernails, wondered if he ought to give Buck a bath. His wife complained yesterday about how Buck smelled. Said he smelled like he'd been *in* something. / Over in T.R., Andrew, the church janitor, walked out to his pigpen carrying a bucket of slop for the pigs. He poured the slop into the trough. His three pigs grunted and slurped. He noticed that the little one had gotten almost as big as the middle one. It was just amazing how animals, with the blessing of God, could grow so fast. He imagined a taste of freshly cooked hot sausage, with egg and hot biscuits, remembered how his uncle wouldn't eat cucumbers because pigs ate them, he said. / Little Steve lay in the feed room on a tight bag of feed, resting on his back, pretending he was on a ship rocking in the ocean. He rolled off one bag and onto another. He heard somebody coming across the feed-room porch. It was his daddy. "Time to go," he said. "Can we stay a little bit longer?" Stephen asked. "No, we got to get on home now." / Train was locking his toolbox and saying to his brother, Luke, "There was this fellow through here from Idaho while you were at lunch, wanted to know if I knew anything about the Civil War. I told him not much. He said six hundred thousand soldiers were killed. Then he said—he said he thought that was a great tribute to the fighting spirit of the American people. I couldn't quite figure that one out." "Well, what the hell do they know in Idaho?" / Vern Goodman was putting his glasses and false teeth in the mailbox where he always put them after work so he wouldn't lose them. It was the only place that worked.

CHURCH WORK

PREACHER CRENSHAW WAS dealing with a son problem. Marjorie generally dealt with the girl things; he dealt with the boy things. "Now, Paul, this is something that I have needed to talk to you about for some time. Love and sweethearts and romance are a gift from God; something He has given us so that we might have children. You, while you were in there in that bathtub, listened to the Devil speak to you. You were unable to say no. This will not be the last time the Devil will tempt you. And I want you to know that the first thing to do now is repent. I will help you. But first, you have to be willing—you have to *want* to repent. Do you want to repent for what you have done?"

"Yessir."

"Truly repent?"

"Yessir."

PAUL LOOKED DOWN and to the side, at the pattern in the rug—something like a bird's head. He twisted his pajama sleeve in his fingers. He had tightened up inside so that no hurt would get through. He had been caught doing a dreadful sin. He had tightened up all over. The colors he saw in the rug were red and yellow.

"Truly repent means you won't do it anymore," his father said.

"Yessir."

"Do you realize you said that *before?*"

"Yessir."

"Well, then, bow your head with me. Dear God, please look down upon this house and bless us and imbue us with Thy spirit. We have all sinned and come short of Thy commandments. Paul, here tonight, has misused his sex. He has played with himself in ways that do not respect his body as a temple of the Holy Spirit, and thus he has committed an act against You. He has repented to me and now he will repent to You. In Jesus' blessed name. Paul?"

"Dear God, I'm sorry for what I did. Thank you for Jesus

and for all the blessings we have. Bless the sick and afflicted all over the world. I repent for all my sins, especially the one tonight. In Jesus' name, amen."

"Dear God, hear our prayer. Bless us and keep us. In Thy holy name, amen. Now son, stand up, pull down your pants and turn around."

BEA BLAINE SAID to Mae Blaine as they sat in their places in their sitting room, "We need to put down some planks between here and the chicken pen. You trucked in some mud again."

"I don't think it was me," said Mae. She was knitting. She thought Bea's face looked more and more like a skull—it was a thought that would emerge to be fought down.

Bea said, "I don't know who else it could of been. I wipe my feet every time."

"I do mine, too."

"You could forget."

"I guess I could."

"I didn't track in the mud."

They were quiet for a minute.

"Mama wouldn't no more allowed mud in the house than a snake," said Bea.

"Wonder what she'd thought of Claude T.?"

"Lord knows she wouldn't have liked that car and that big

ring. That is just too much. I wonder if Dorothea has said any-thing to him about all that."

"I doubt it. Come on up here, Kitty." Mae lifted her knit-ting, waited, and then set it back down on the cat's back. "I been thinking. You think Dorothea will get buried beside Claude T., or us?"

"I don't know. I have thought about it."

"Well, I have, too. Every now and then."

"She lived with us a lot longer than him. People are get-ting bad all over the place about moving off and forgetting family. That fellow in the yellow shirt has got kin over in T.R. and there he is—lived all over everywhere and won't even stay with them and no telling what kind of hardships his fam-ily's been through with him gone off somewhere."

"What yellow shirt?" asked Mae.

"The one staying at the Settle Inn—with the pencil-thin mustache. And if Claude T. moved off somewhere you know Dorothea would go with him. I don't know what it's all com-ing to."

"Did you hear that cricket?"

"No. I might have heard one outside."

"I'm talking about in the bedroom."

"No. There's not a cricket in there. It was outside."

"Listen. Did you hear that?"

"That was outside," said Bea.

"I don't think so. I think it was right in there in the bedroom."

"No it wadn't."

"The thought of trying to find that thing. Just wait until you get in there. You'll hear him then."

"There ain't no cricket in there."

UMSTEAD PULLED UP to the Pendergrass Grill. No cars in the parking lot, but lights were on inside. The screen door slammed behind him. The lights were bright and a young woman, mighty attractive young thing, was wiping off a table. "Y'all closed?" he asked.

She looked at a clock over the door. "Not until eight. We can fix you up something."

"I just want half a hot dog with slaw and peanuts on it, half a pack of Juicy Fruit chewing gum, and a Coca-Cola."

She picked up a tray with plates and glasses. "We don't serve chewing gum except on Tuesday."

"Then make it a hamburger all the way and a Pepsi. Y'all don't sell beer, do you?"

"Nosir." Cheryl moved toward the back. "One burger, all the way," she said to the kitchen. "That's pretty funny," she said to Umstead.

"Coming up," came a woman's voice from the kitchen.

Umstead looked around. Pictures hanging on the walls—
some men holding big fish. Checkered curtains. Electric
cords running up to lighted 7-Up and Pepsi signs. A clean
feel. Polished wood.

"There's your Pepsi. It'll be just a minute on your hamburger."

"I got all night . . . but I'll try to be out of here by eight,
so you can go home and get some rest."

"I just live right out there."

"Oh, you must be . . . ? What's your daddy's name?"

"Johnny Daniels."

"That's right. I used to live over the other side of T.R. and
I'm kind of passing through, visiting some relatives. I used to
come over here to Listre years ago."

"Welcome back."

"Thank you. Seems like I remember you got a big brother
—or sister?"

"Brother. He's in Memphis now. I got a little brother
here."

"That's right. I don't think he was born when I left. Well,
I know he won't."

"He ain't but seven."

"Order up," the woman in back called.

"That Mrs. Pendergrass back there?"

"Yessir."

" 'Sir?' Don't call me 'sir.' Makes me feel old."

"I'm sorry. What's your name then?"

"I'm Delbert Jones. My pleasure. And what's your name?"

"Cheryl. Cheryl Daniels. Here you go. Burger all the way. Maybe you ain't all that old."

"I ain't. Listen, I been aiming to ask somebody—how does that old bulldog over at the gas station tell the weather?"

"Trouble. Depends on where he . . . Trouble. That's his name. Depends on where he takes his morning nap. If it's inside, it's going to rain. Don't let them bet you over there. They've won money on it."

OVER IN HER office, Mrs. Clark tucked a clean white sheet around the couch cushions. She swallowed several of her capsules with a cup of water, smoothed her hand over the sheet. She felt the very presence of Jesus Christ of Nazareth. The Lord, in His house. The sheets were so clean and white.

In the bathroom she hooked the latch and took off all her clothes and draped them on a chair. Just like at home, this was something she could do the very same way every time.

> *I come to the garden alone,*
> *While the dew is still on the roses.*

And the voice I hear, falling on my ear,
The Son of God discloses.

She dried off real good with the towel Claude T. had brought.

Back in her office, in her pajamas, she hooked her door, then looked through the window down at the blinker light, blinking yellow, lay down on her back on the clean sheet, feeling all clean. She pulled her sheet and blanket over her.

"Dear Lord," she prayed aloud, "thank you for our county, and state, and the United States, and our North American continent. We pray for the sick . . ."

ON HIS THIRD try, Jack Umstead found an outside church door that was open. About one in two churches had one door open somewhere, and very often there was a stocked refrigerator in a church, sometimes a full kitchen, with crackers and canned goods. And he wasn't beyond going through a trash can or two if there'd been a chicken dinner the night before. You could find whole chicken wings completely untouched, sometimes fried and/or barbecued. They'd keep for up to a week. And with his suit, white shirt, and his tie, he knew damned well he could talk his way out of any difficulty.

As he stepped into a kind of small office-library room, he

heard a voice behind a closed door: " . . . and we pray for all babies without mothers. We're thankful for our earth, our solar system, the Milky Way, everything in the universe, our beautiful moon, and the universe itself. Help us to love one another and to love Jesus and accept Him as our Lord and Saviour. In Jesus' name, amen."

SHE HEARD STEPS, quiet steps in the library room out there—approaching her door. Dear Lord, she thought. Could that . . . ? It wasn't Mr. Crenshaw's walk, or the janitor Andrew's, or Claude T.'s, and they were the only ones who . . . It was a very soft walk. Could that . . . be . . . ? His Own Self? Here in His own house? Did *He* live here sometimes? Too? Should she . . . should she speak?

"Jesus?"

"Yes."

"Oh, Jesus. Is that *You,* Jesus?"

"Verily, verily, it is. For God so loved the world He gave His only begotten son that whosoever believeth in Him should not perish but have everlasting life. All is well. Do not be afraid. I am, ah, come to save the world."

She heard a chair being pulled up to the door. This could not be. But what if it *was?* He'd said *believe.* "Dear Jesus, I have hurt myself. And I'm having to spend a few days in Thy house.

I have . . . I have bathed and come to bed." But he would already know all that. She took a deep breath. She didn't want to faint now. This was really happening.

"Okay with me," said the voice—said Jesus. "Good bathing is a good habit. Did you brush your teeth?"

"I brush them every morning with baking soda."

She had dreamed and dreamed of walking in the garden with Him, alone, but she'd always believed she'd have to die first and go to heaven. Now she was actually talking to Him through a closed door at the church and it was taking her breath. It was all true. The Bible was true. God was true. She felt a little faint. So what if she did faint? It wouldn't make any difference now. It was all true. This might be the very beginning of the very end of the world. The end of Time, with heaven waiting, waiting for her and all the other Christians, dead or alive, to ascend up into heaven itself.

"Make yourself at home," said the voice. "And what would . . . what would thy name be?"

"I am Dorothea—Mrs. Claude T. Clark. I am Thy servant, oh Lord. Did you hear my prayer, oh Lord?"

"I sure did. It was a mighty good prayer, too. I don't get too many that good."

Dorothea tried to picture the face behind the voice. She never liked hair on a man's face, but she'd never questioned

Jesus' right to have it. Then it struck her that He might *not* have a beard. All that had gone on so long ago when customs were different. "Jesus, do you have a beard?"

"No, I don't, Dorothea. I do have a mustache, though. I, ah, shave when I come to America."

"Well, I'm glad, but I also try to understand the customs of the Middle Ages, Jesus. And, Jesus, I've always tried to be a good person."

"And you have been. You have been a good person, Dorothea. One of the best in this church. You've always done real good. I'm proud of you. *Mr.* Clark had problems, though, before he died . . . no, he hasn't, he hasn't died, has he?"

"That's right, he *hasn't*." That proved it was Jesus. He *knew*. "And I knew he had problems, Lord. Claude T. just got too interested in money, Lord."

"You can call me Jesus."

"Yes . . . thank you, Jesus. He just got too interested in money . . . Didn't he, Jesus?"

"Money is not something that is very important, Mrs. Clark. As you know. I don't even carry none with me anymore. Love is what is important. Love thy neighbor as thyself. Love thine enemy. But sometimes I do need to get a little money to live on. Love won't buy a fruit pie and a Pepsi, you know—something Jesus needs, too—and so I usually just stop by a church, a Baptist church is always a good bet." Dorothea thought about the preacher's discretionary fund, looked over at her desk.

"And while I'm at it," said Jesus, "is there a little money in there, say a five or ten, that you could slide under the door? Better not open the door. I have to depend on the kind hearts of, ah, fellow Christians for money. Fellow Baptists. I'm just like everybody else, more or less, when I'm on earth."

"Well, yes, there's Brother Crenshaw's discretionary fund." His mind was working right with hers. "Let me just get it. This is Your money, Lord—Your house and everything in it. Let me get up here."

Right to thirty-five, back around past thirty-five to five, back right to sixteen; the big envelope with Mr. Crenshaw's discretionary money in it. Her hands shook. Her ankle was hurting. She got out two fives, hobbled to the door, dropped them, and pushed them, one bill at a time, with her cane—it was hard with those four little feet—under the door. She had a sudden urge. She flicked back the hook, grabbed the door handle, turned it, pulled.

It pulled back, with some force.

"Whoa, there, Mrs. Clark. My face might . . . might blind you, I'm afraid. Sometimes that happens."

"Certainly, Lord."

"Maybe next time we can work something out. Some kind of protection for your eyes."

"Yes, Jesus. Yes, I can understand that. I'm sorry. Oh, Jesus, my favorite song is 'In the Garden.' And I want you to know I slapped Claude T.'s hand over and over."

"I remember 'In the Garden.' I sure do. I remember that one. Lovely song. *I walk through the garden alone, while the da da da da da da da,* and Claude T.'s hand needed slapping. Good for you. And how long you reckon you're going to be stuck in here?"

"Oh, Lord, I don't know. Will you come back? I'll be here for a while with this ankle. Could you . . . ? Dear Lord, could you heal my ankle?—if you got time. It's all right if you can't."

"Mrs. Clark, I can't heal your ankle—I just don't do that kind of thing much anymore, but you been so good I might be able to work something out. You keep that ankle elevated, and don't say anything about me dropping in, if you don't mind. You know. Anything. Maybe I could speed up the healing some. But if you tell anybody about this, some of God's plans could get messed up. Not that He couldn't straighten them back out, but you know what I mean. I'll be back real soon, probably tomorrow night. Don't tell anybody, because as soon as you do I'll have to leave town. Now, may peace be with you."

"Jesus, I don't mean to talk bad about Claude T. He's a good man at heart. He's been real good to me. I don't want to give the wrong impression."

"Claude T. *is* a good man. He sure is. Don't you worry about Claude T. Claude T. does have a good heart down beneath everything."

She had always suspected that.

UMSTEAD WALKED TO his car. He wished he had a buddy around that he could tell all that to. Telling a buddy— reminded him of that joke: Man on a desert island. Been there for years and years. He sees somebody struggling in the water. Saves her life. Turns out to be Rosalind Russell. Rosalind takes all her clothes off, says, "You saved my life. I'll do anything for you." He says, "Let's go to my little shack over there and make love for a week." She says, "Okay." They do, and at the end of the week she says, "I'm so happy you saved my life. Is there anything else I can do? I just feel like I ought to do something else." He says, "Yeah, you can pretend you're my fishing buddy, Bob." She says, "What!?" He says, "Yes. Please. Put on this hat and coat, go stand under that tree." She says, "Well, okay," and does. He walks over, puts his arm around her shoulder, looks her in the eye, says, "Bob, old buddy, you ain't gonna believe this, but Rosalind Russell has been choking my chicken for a solid week."

He needed some kind of buddy. Maybe that Luke down at the service station. Or better still, Train. Train could keep a secret. That was pretty clear by just looking at him.

As he pulled his Buick out onto the road, he looked over at the parsonage. Now, there—in there—was a man with some power. A whole community cooking him chicken and stew beef, and him having to work just on Sundays for half a day, and visit the hospital once in a while. Selling God. But the man sure was not free. He was locked in that house and all, with other people—a damn family. But on the other hand, maybe he was one of the Christians who went all the way, the whole nine yards.

He approached the blinker light—blinking yellow. It was like it was saying a little something to him, but he couldn't figure out exactly what. Nobody could.

STEPHEN ESCORTED HIS mother up the long stairs from the church basement to the quiet hymn-book-smelling first floor behind the giant room with pews. They were near the narrow door where the choir members entered the choir place. You could go through another door into the big room with all the pews, walk over close to the high mighty wood thing the preacher stood behind, and the two giant chairs up there. You could walk up on the stage and look out there where all the people would be sitting on Sunday. Now, today, with everybody gone, the silence would be God's breath. To be in there without all the people was like a secret.

They walked through the little library of books and pamphlets about church things and on into Mrs. Clark's office.

"Alease, it's mighty nice of you to come over here to do this."

"I thought you might like a little something to eat, too," said Alease. She put down a piece of pound cake wrapped in wax paper beside some other food already on a little table.

"Sit down . . . Son, why don't you sit on that stool over there. I declare, you're turning into such a fine young man. I appreciate you thinking about me, Alease. People have been so nice. You know, there were a few things said when I stayed in here last winter, but I was just doing the best I could. I couldn't do anything other than what I did."

Stephen couldn't quite figure it out. It looked like she was living in there—a pair of bedroom shoes over there. And a jar of stuff women put on their face at night.

"Alease, I have felt so close to Jesus, and Alease, I've got to tell you, I've just got to tell you. I've got to tell you that"—Mrs. Clark leaned forward—"I had a visit from Jesus. He came. He really did."

Stephen remembered that new man. His Sunday school teacher said Jesus would dress different in modern times. "Did he have on a yellow shirt?" asked Stephen.

"I don't know. I couldn't see him."

"Honey," his mother said, "that's not what Mrs. Clark is talking about. She's talking about something in her mind, in her prayer. Here, Dorothea, let me get your feet up here so I can get to those toenails. Is it going to be all right to work on your foot with that sprained ankle?"

"I think it will. But, no. No, I *am* talking about the real Jesus, Alease. Standing right outside that door. It was Jesus His own self. I just have to believe it was."

"Well, that's good," said his mother. She was getting her clippers and file out of her pocketbook. "That's good."

"But I shouldn't be talking about it."

Stephen watched as his mother removed Mrs. Clark's shoes, then started in on the old lady's toenails. The big toenail on one foot was yellow and looked like a big cornflake.

"That little toe toenail on my right foot ain't come back yet."

"It sure hadn't. Stephen, do you want to try to cut one? You wouldn't mind, would you, Mrs. Clark?"

"Oh, no. Long as he's careful."

"Do you want to, Stephen?"

"Yes ma'am."

"Better let your mama do the big one," said Mrs. Clark. "You do the second one, maybe."

"But watch me do this one first," said his mama. "We want to be real careful."

Stephen remembered what his mama's feet and toenails looked like. He remembered his daddy's, Uncle Raleigh's, Mrs. Clark's, Miss Bea's, Miss Mae's, and his own. His own toes were bland little faces, his mama's were good, and one time she let him paint them red, his daddy's were careful and a little bit afraid and real white, Uncle Raleigh's were red and messed up, Miss Bea's and Miss Mae's were the same—very mashed together, with Miss Bea's long second toes—and Mrs. Clark's had the cornflake and the one without any toenail at all. Every foot was a little community without a blinker light. He had cut one of his mama's toenails one time and one of his daddy's three or four times and it was very pleasing, like sweeping lines of dirt into the dustpan. Like picking a old, dry, heavy scab. Like sitting on the grocery porch and drinking a Big Top grape. Like being a fireman or a cowboy. Like hearing the story of David and Goliath. Like baseball. Like cowboys killing Indians.

THE COLLISION STORY

JUST AFTER DAYLIGHT the next morning, Jack Umstead sat in his chair near cabin 6 at the Settle Inn. He couldn't sleep in the mornings, but he could sit beside a road and watch cars pass. Their front ends looked like faces—Studebakers with great big noses, Fords with pop eyes and regular mouths, Chevrolets, Buicks, and Oldsmobiles with turned-down fish mouths. He knew the year, make, and model of every single one.

Umstead had this theory: Animals had all these mental nerves that told them what to do, what to be afraid of—what not to do so they wouldn't end up dead. And people had mental nerves that got developed back when they lived like animals, and these mental nerves kept working past the time they were actually needed. And what one of those mental nerves said was: If you see anything that moves across the ground, you'd better look at it in the face to figure out if it will eat you up. And this is why cars looked like they had faces.

Umstead watched a good-sized black kitten walking along the top of a low rock wall that was beside his cabin. The kitten jumped down from the wall, crossed the road, and entered the woods cautious-like. Now a tiger, Umstead thought, will eat you up, but it has a very calm face. What about that? Well, not if it's real mad, showing its teeth. But then an elephant looks about the same all the time, except it probably throws its ears back. And a horse. But you do get a feeling about *people* by looking in their faces, and that's why that mental nerve has lasted, and cars look like they've got faces. There's two eyes: two headlights. One mouth: one grille. Why did the carmakers decide to have two headlights instead of three? Mental nerves had something to do with it.

In thirty minutes he looked at his watch again and stood to head for breakfast at the grill. There was nothing much he liked better than two over easy, chopped and mixed with grits for a toast dip, bacon, hot black coffee, and cold orange juice, all while he read the newspaper and found something to talk to somebody about. To Cheryl, maybe.

At the end of the fence he stopped. A little boy and what

must be his mama were coming out onto the front porch of the first house there. It was the boy that . . . the grocery store kid. Toomey. He could tell somehow that the mama was what . . . religious? She had that look about her, but there was also something else. Something he liked. Something he liked a lot. Her hair had some of that deep dark red in it, something that said . . . said she'd be hard to get through to, but once he did, she'd turn loose. Maybe that was it.

Besides faces, this business of reading people had to do with the way people moved, the way they walked, and how long they looked at you at a time. Scientists would figure it out one day. Scientists would figure out how—well, like that Redding fellow, Blake: eyes close together, no chin. That was for sure not the person who owned the gas station. That was the face of a helper, somebody without any sense of leadership. You could see right away that Train was the commander. A man with a jaw. And eyes that didn't give away the first thing. A man Umstead wouldn't mind getting to know a little bit. A man he probably had a lot in common with as far as deep character and intelligence was concerned.

The little boy climbed up into the porch swing, turned, and plopped down. The mother, she would be Mrs. Toomey then, held a plate of food and a fork. She pulled up a porch chair to a spot in front of the swing and pushed the swing, forked some egg, gave the swing another little push, held the fork out toward the boy, and looked out across the yard. The house was nice, not too simple, a little complicated-looking with a lot of flowers in the yard and up next to the house.

"Come here, little pig," she said, loud. "Come here, little pig. I got you something to eat, little pig. You come here, now. Get you something to eat."

Umstead watched the boy swing forward and mouth the egg. Damn.

The mother, still looking out toward the road: "Come on, little pig. Come on now. I got you some . . . *What in the world happened to your food, little pig!?*"

The little boy about shit a brick. Having one hell of a time. There was a woman who didn't need no instruction about how to get food down a child.

"MAMA, THERE'S A man."

"That's okay. He's just walking down to the blinker light."

"That's the man at the store. He got a penny out from behind my ear." And he talked ugly, Stephen thought.

The man stopped.

Stephen's mother lifted her hand and smiled. The hand held the fork with egg on it.

"Where'd you get all them pigs?" said the man.

"Oh, they just come up here every morning for breakfast."

"There's some right pretty ones out there. They look hungry, too."

"Somebody keeps getting their food."

"Well, good luck. I'm going to get a bite myself."

"He might be a gypsy," said Stephen.

"No, I don't think so."

"He lives at the Settle Inn."

"That don't mean you're a gypsy, son. You can stay at the Settle Inn and not be a gypsy."

UMSTEAD HAD A notion to go running across the yard toward them, screaming, "Oink, oink!" He walked on. If he did that he'd just scare them. But there could be some pleasure in that, too. He wondered how many people in the history of the world, if any, had been pretending to feed imaginary pigs, when all of a sudden real pigs showed up. Now that was a question nobody could ever answer, no matter what, even though the answer was as *really there* as answers to easy questions like the number of blinker lights in the world, or how many times that blinker light had blinked so far—you could figure that one out—but not one like how many people a day in the world, on average, thought about a tree while they farted, or when they were having supper two weeks ago. What percentage thought about a bare tree, what percentage about a leafy tree? Which year since 1850 had more leaves fall off trees? That just showed you about knowledge. There was a lot going on you didn't know about.

> Little Kenny Rollins stood in his bathroom a half-mile away. He held his penis in both hands and looked down as he repeatedly pulled open the little hole with his thumbs and then pushed it back together. "Hello there, Kenny," Kenny said. "My name is Mr. Knob-knob. I'm a lumberjack." "Hello, Mr. Knob-knob. How do you feel today?" "I feel just fine. I'm a-looking me some trees to cut down." "Oh? Well, I know where some trees are. Why don't you come with me?" "Okay, Kenny. I believe I will."

Umstead, walking toward the blinker light, checked his watch, counted the blinks for ten seconds: twelve. Twelve times three, thirty-six. Thirty-six times two, seventy-two. The same as heartbeats a minute.

All the stores except the sisters' probably for sure took their stash home and then probably to the bank. More and more people were using banks. There might even be a stash at the little boy's house on some weekend nights—that his daddy brought home from the grocery store.

He'd go with his original plan. He'd wait until the next storm and break in downstairs at the Blaine sisters'. In the meantime, he'd get more or less comfortable.

Inside the grill he found Cheryl waiting on a mama, daddy, and two kids. He went to the counter where he'd be close to the cash register and could talk to her. He got a newspaper from a chair, sat down.

"What'll it be, Mr. Jones?" said Cheryl. She was behind the counter waiting to write on her order pad.

"Call me Delbert. You make me feel like a old man. I'll take two over easy, grits, bacon, toast, orange juice, and coffee. Bacon crisp, if I got a choice. You work all day?"

"I get off late mornings and in the afternoon."

"I see."

Through the order window, "Two over, crisp bacon, toast." Then to Umstead, "We got some mighty good fresh biscuits."

"I ain't never been real big on biscuits for some reason."

"I might have to give you one anyway. You ain't ever had none like these."

"Give me two."

She set a cup of coffee and a glass of orange juice in front of him, turned, and he looked at her rear end move, apron strings falling down across those just pure-t perfect hips, and under that smooth white skirt: a panties outline.

She placed a dish with two biscuits, butter, and grape jelly in front of him.

"Thank you." He could get used to this.

MIDMORNING, UMSTEAD WAS sitting outside on the bench at Train's when Train himself rolled out in his wheelchair. Umstead had never seen him outside before. He was somebody who didn't pretend to be a Christian.

"Trouble," said Train. "Sic . . . *sic.*"

The old squatty bulldog grunted, got up slowly, hobbled around the side of the building, out of sight.

"What's he going after?" asked Umstead.

"Just getting his exercise."

"I see . . . looks like it's gone be a scorcher." Umstead needed to be careful here. He didn't say anything for a while. "You fix radios, huh? Besides running this place."

"Yeah, I try."

"Hobby, more or less?"

"Yeah."

They sat for a little while. Trouble came in view from the

other side of the building, slowly waddled along, lay down in front of his box, and grunted.

"You seen one of them televisions?" said Umstead.

"Yeah, I saw one."

"They say they're expecting to sell a bunch of them in the next year or so. They're pretty interesting. I wonder if they work like a radio."

"I don't know."

Casey Odell drove up, went inside, came back out with a Coke, and sat on a stack of drink crates. "Man, I tell you one thing. It's hot. Train, how you been?"

"I was feeling okay until I got up this morning."

"My name's Casey Odell."

Umstead reached over, shook his hand. "Delbert Jones."

"Oh yeah, you the one down at the Settle Inn."

"That's right."

"Where you from?"

"Mississippi. Just visiting some of my kinfolks. I lived the other side of T.R. for a spell when I was little. I'm just kind of heading home. Had some time off from work."

"Well, this ain't a bad place to settle—is it, Train?"

"Nope."

"I do remember the stores around here," said Umstead, "and I remember there was a sawmill somewhere, wadn't there?"

"Up that rise behind the flintrock over there," said Casey. "That thing finally burned down back in . . . when was that, Train?"

"Thirty-nine."

"Thirty-nine. That was the last big fire around here before your tires burned up, won't it?"

"Far as I know."

Umstead wanted to find out more about the Blaine sisters — whether or not they used a bank. "Wadn't there some talk about opening a bank around here?" He looked at Train. Maybe he shouldn't have said that.

Train looked at him. "Not that I've heard of."

"That might have been someplace else," said Umstead. "I've lived in right many places over the last four or five years. I work for a surveying company down in Mississippi. Some of these little intersections get to reminding me of one another."

"When did you leave out of here?" said Casey.

"Oh, must have been, let's see, early twenties. I was just a little kid. Old man Blaine had his store over there. I remember that. I can't remember much more, except I remember the sawmill. Them sisters were over there at the store back then too, I think."

"I tell you one thing. They've *always* been there, ain't they, Train?" said Casey.

137

"Pretty much."

"They tended to their mama for a long time after their daddy died," said Casey. "I remember him. He took to sitting outside under that little shelter over the door and died one day sitting out there in the chair and they never told their mama. She lived another I think four years. They took care of her like a baby down in the back part of that store."

"What you reckon that is about the thunderstorms?" asked Umstead. He wanted to be sure they were gone during thunderstorms.

"That business of the thunderstorms is Mae's problem mostly, what I've always heard," said Casey, "afraid of lightning and thunder. That came up after their little brother got killed on the railroad is what I've always heard, hadn't you, Train?"

"He got dragged something like a quarter-mile underneath a train in a bad storm," said Train. "One night, summer night. And lived for some number of days after it happened. Where'd you drive in from?" Train asked Umstead.

Why did he want to know that? Umstead wondered. "I was visiting a army buddy of mine in Richmond right before I left to drive down here. Fellow with one eye—had a shell go off in his rifle chamber."

"What road did you live on, other side of T.R.?"

"We lived on the Old Sloan Road across the county line. You know that road?" Need to get off this.

"I do."

"On across the county line. We lived back in there. We didn't have no mule-truck collisions, though. How'd that happen? I never got in on the details."

"Oh man, I tell you one thing," said Casey. "That was something. Boy I remember that. It was a Saturday afternoon and Butch Gaylord had hired Chuckie Freeman to plow out that field over there. Right over there. Anyway—you want to tell it, Train?"

"Go ahead."

"Well, Chuckie needed the money bad and wadn't in no notion to let on about how little he knew about plowing. He felt bad about it all. Still does. He's told you how bad he feels about it, ain't he, Train?"

"Yep."

"Well, the mule was ornery and after a couple of rows she took out for home, which placed her headed that way along the road there—at a right fast clip, dragging the plow along. Chuckie just gave up and let her go. He didn't know much about mules."

"He didn't know nothing about mules," said Train.

"Coming from the other way was Train and his brother,

Ralph. Ralph was driving their daddy's old Ford wide open and Train was right behind him driving this new truck of *his*. You was *both* bad about driving fast, actually, won't you, Train?" said Casey.

"Well, yeah."

"I've heard you say so more than once. Anyway, Train passed Ralph about time they got to the church down there, coming this way."

Umstead thought about how the back door to the Blaine sisters' store was out of sight of everything, and hell, even if they *were* in there, two old women couldn't put up no fight.

"Mule's name was Molly," said Casey.

"Dolly," said Train.

"That's right, it was. Why don't you tell it, Train?"

"Naw, go ahead."

"Once Train got completely around Ralph, them and the mule was all on the same side of the road, Molly still on the——"

"Dolly."

"Dolly, shit, still on the shoulder, coming right at them. And them right at her. The mule *turned* right in front of the truck to cross the road at her normal crossing place, see, doing this little trot with her head up, and dragging that plow, and they say Train never even hit the brakes—and Train you don't remember nothing about it do you?"

"Nope."

"Ralph always says Dolly decided to do two things at once, he says: 'Number one, try to jump whatever it was coming at her, and number two, shit.' Near as we could tell— see I was sitting over there at the flintrock and I heard it and I was—"

"What did it sound like?" asked Umstead. "Mule-truck head-on?" Now how many of them had happened since trucks come on the market?

"Well, I tell you. It sounded . . . it sounded more or less like a mule-truck head-on is about all I can say. Kind of this loud *Ka-whomp.*"

Train took it: "My hood ornament and the whole front center of the hood hit her shoulder and knocked her front end out from under her, and she busted in through the windshield ass first and stuck there, with that plow whipping around and lodging in behind the right door, and the truck rolled once when it hit the ditch, broke Dolly's neck—they said, as if she wadn't already dead—and dropped me in Gus White's yard unconscious, and mule shit all over my face and shoulders, and after I was *out* for ten, fifteen minutes and then come to, they *said* for the next two hours, which I don't remember, they *said* I kept asking what happened, over and over. I'd say, 'What happened?' and they'd say, 'You hit a mule widge your truck,' and I'd say, 'Naw,' and they'd say, 'Oh, yeah,' and in five minutes I'd say, 'What happened?' and they'd say, 'You hit a mule widge your truck,' and I'd say, 'Naw,' and they'd say, 'Oh, yeah.'"

Once he gets cranked up, thought Umstead, he talks right along.

"One bad thing," said Casey. "Now I can tell this because you were unconscious. One bad thing was that all mixed in with that mule shit was crushed-up windshield glass. Chuckie tried to wipe off Train's face with a towel but of course it cut him up. We'd all run down there, see. Now I saw that part. There, you can see the scars. Turn your head a little bit, Train."

"Yeah," said Umstead. "I'd heard about all that but never heard the specifics."

"He broke his ankle so bad," said Casey, "it made his leg shorter and that could have kept him out of the army but he wanted to serve his country and so ended up taking that Jap bullet through the spine."

"'A great tribute to the fighting spirit of the American people,'" said Train.

"Severed it," said Casey. "Just like you'd do a wishbone."

Train looked at Casey. "Where'd you come up with that?"

"Well, you the one said it was severed."

"That's right. I am. I can talk about my own accidents, Casey. My own injuries."

"I'm sorry."

"Yeah, I heard something about that one, too," said Umstead. "'Cept I didn't know it was a *Jap* bullet. That's too bad."

They were silent.

"We got a right good little community here," said Train, looking at Umstead. "People are pretty settled and we don't have much trouble."

"I like it here."

"It's a good little community. What are your plans?"

"Oh, I don't know. I'm trying to work out a few things on the telephone with my cousin over in Summerlin. She just come in from Baltimore and we got some family troubles I think'll work out all right in a week or two if we don't rush it. I've pretty much learned the value of patience."

"I don't know any white Joneses other side of T.R.," said Casey.

"They're right good ways out, most of them, and there ain't nobody left much, except my cousins and a few more."

"What was your mama's name?" asked Train.

"Her name was Beulah and my cousin's name is Annie."

"Seems like I heard of a Annie Jones," said Casey.

"Yeah, I think there's probably more than one."

CHICKEN'S EYE

SEVERAL TIMES MISS Mae Blaine had invited Stephen over to sit for a spell. He would sit outside in the metal chair beside the long, low icebox. Miss Mae would open the lid and scratch a line on a big block of ice with the ice pick for a customer. The line would be in the right place for a nickel or dime or quarter block of ice. Then she'd hand Stephen the ice pick and he'd chip along her line until a block just the right size fell off. There might be some fresh chickens in there too —no heads, little doodie things for necks, cold, the color of his wrist on the inside.

Miss Bea might come up behind him and say, "Pinch him. Pinch that chicken and watch him jump." But he wouldn't pinch it.

Miss Mae would sit in the rocker and talk to him: "The Good Book says for you to mind your mama and daddy. The Good Book says for you not to ever steal anything, not to never tell a story, not even a little story, to do unto others as you would have them do unto you. The Good Book says believe in the Lord Jesus Christ and thou shall be saved. The Good Book says . . ."

One day Miss Mae had to go inside and Miss Bea sat down and looked him in the eyes and said, "Don't you ever play with yourself, you hear me, and since you don't have no brothers and sisters, you're going to have to take care of your mama and daddy. Do you understand that?"

"Yes ma'am."

"Somebody might try to take you away from your mama and daddy. Do you understand that?"

"No ma'am . . . Yes ma'am."

"Well, you better understand it. Don't you ever leave your mama and daddy, do you hear me?"

"Yes ma'am."

"Now, do you want to learn how to shoot a chicken?"

"Yes ma'am, I think so."

"You're going to be our helper-outer. Follow me on down to the chicken pen and I'll show you how. Go tell your daddy first." Stephen wondered if the skin around her ribs was maybe green. He went to the door of the grocery and told his daddy what Miss Bea wanted.

His daddy came out on the store porch and Miss Bea said over to him, "Remember I told you I was going to hire your son to be our chicken shooter?"

"Yes ma'am."

"The time is here."

"Oh, well, okay. You mean now?"

"Right now. This minute."

"Let's go, son. I'll go with you."

Amongst the chickens, Stephen watched as Miss Bea picked one walking straight away from her. "If you do it from the side," she said, "then she's apt to walk off. So you get behind her, you save some time. Watch me." The chicken stepped away, bobbing its head. Miss Bea stepped closer, put the gun to her shoulder, aimed, and pulled the trigger. The gun clicked. She handed Stephen the gun while still holding on to it, pulling back the hammer and helping him raise the stock to his shoulder. The shotgun was heavy and had an adventure in it and some kind of death.

"Just practice aiming a little bit there," she said. Then to his daddy. "He needs to learn to shoot a gun and my aim ain't getting no better."

"Yes'um, I was planning on teaching him pretty soon."

"He ever shot a shotgun?"

"No, not yet."

HARVEY WANTED TO be taking care of this matter of his son shooting a shotgun for the first time. Both these women at one time or another seemed to him a little bit off, somehow. They sure were different from his mama, who always stayed in the house and did all her work in there—until she got sick, and now she just sat in her chair or lay in her bed in his sister's living room while they all took care of her and brought her snuff and chocolate-covered cherries every once in a while and listened to her say things they all repeated to one another. She, like his father, was one of the wisest people on earth and all the offspring knew that and knew to treat them that way, so harmony could prevail.

"Can I shoot the rooster?" Stephen asked.

"We don't shoot the rooster," said Miss Bea. "We need him for his services."

The comment troubled Harvey. It was about sex, spoken in the wide open. He laughed a little laugh, half funny, half worry.

STEPHEN LOOKED FROM chicken head to chicken head. Some of the chickens had little tender-looking red skins hanging from their chins and head. Little dribble things. None of them would look at him. They'd look off, and then if you got too close, bob away with high steps. One of them looked kind of wise. Stephen didn't want to shoot that one. "Which one?" he asked. It was almost like they were people. They could even be people in the Bible. Or people from the city.

"I'll show you which one in a minute," said Miss Bea.

His daddy said, "She'll flap around all over the place once you shoot her. Don't let it scare you." Then his daddy said to Miss Bea, "He won't much over three when Papa got rid of all his chickens."

Stephen looked and saw the new man in the yellow shirt, the gypsy man, Mr. Jones, walking down there. He figured Mr. Jones would start talking, telling a funny story or something. His daddy would more or less stand quiet.

"Is that a four-ten?" asked Mr. Jones.

"Sure is," said Miss Bea. "Little Steve's going to be my chicken shooter. A penny a chicken, and he's about to shoot his first one."

The big people were watching him. Stephen eyed a chicken, a white chicken. The white ones might be connected to God or Jesus. He remembered getting run at by a great big old mean rooster when he was at his granddaddy's house one time. If *this* rooster came at him and the gun was loaded he could shoot it right in the face.

"He ever shot a shotgun before?" Mr. Jones asked his daddy.

"I was aiming to teach him before his next birthday."

"Go ahead and practice, son," said Miss Bea. "Just aim right down the barrel and pull the trigger. Lift it right up to your shoulder. Get up close to their head but come in from the rear, now, else they'll shy away from you."

Stephen brought the gun up to his shoulder and started for a nearby chicken. The chicken darted behind him and Stephen turned, still holding the gun up to his shoulder, swinging it around toward the onlookers.

Mr. Jones ducked. "Whoa. That's what kills people, Budrow."

"It ain't loaded," said his daddy.

"The gun is not loaded, sir," said Miss Bea to Mr. Jones. "You stick to your business and I'll stick to mine—whatever yours is."

"Son," said his daddy, "don't point the gun at anybody no matter if it's loaded or not."

"It ain't loaded," said Stephen. "She never put the bullet in it."

"It's a shell," said Miss Bea.

"And don't point it at anybody no matter what," said his daddy.

Stephen's ears felt hot. He wanted to go ahead and shoot. He felt just a little bit like he might cry. He wanted to get this on over with. Miss Bea walked up behind a chicken very slowly. He felt like he was getting asthma.

"See there," she said. "Once you get behind him you got a better chanst."

"Why don't you just chop his head off?" said Mr. Jones.

"You got to catch them to do that, and I can't get around like I used to. Pick that one right over there, son. See that one? Walk up right behind her and aim at the back of her head and pull that trigger."

Stephen walked up behind the chicken, kind of aimed, pulled the trigger, which clicked.

"Okay," said Miss Bea. "Now we can load it. Let me see the gun. There we go. Now. I've got the safety on. That's right there. See. Before it'll shoot, you're going to have to push that, like this."

"My grandma used to choke chickens," said Casey Odell, walking up. "Sit down on the ground, get them between her legs, and choke them. That's what she used to do when she got real old."

"I've choked my own chicken," Mr. Jones said to Casey, "but I ain't ever choked nobody else's."

"That reminds me of a joke. These two fellows were . . ."

Stephen held the gun to his shoulder and walked behind the chicken. The chicken took a step, then another step. He brought the gun to his shoulder, aimed, pushed the safety forward, closed his eyes and pulled the trigger. He felt the explosion and kick. He opened his eyes. Chickens were squawking and scattering. The chicken he'd almost hit was climbing onto the backs of two other chickens—all three flapping their wings. He'd missed and blown a hole in the ground.

"You can't close your eyes," said Mr. Jones. "See that little BB on the top of the gun barrel, Budrow? Put the safety back on. Hold it straight——"

"We don't need any help," said Miss Bea. "I already showed him that. You just keep quiet while we take care of this, now why don't you, sir."

Miss Bea held the gun to Stephen's shoulder. "Look through that V and get that BB right in the V and hold it there and be sure the BB looks like it's right on the chicken's head. Then pull the trigger. That's right. See, you got the little V, then the BB, and that makes it pointed at something. Keep the BB in the V and the BB on the chicken head. That's all you do." She took the gun, loaded it, handed it back to Stephen, who got behind a chicken, brought the gun up, aimed, and pulled the trigger. KA-BLAOW.

The chicken had no head and blood was there. Its wings

beat so hard it raised dust. It flapped and bounced in a circle, then straight for Stephen. He tried to step away from it but it tumbled against his leg. He stepped back. The chicken shivered, then lay still.

"Bull's-eye," said Casey Odell.

"Chicken's eye," said Mr. Jones. "That took about a hour longer than it needed to."

"I think it took about the right time," said Miss Bea.

"The right time for you."

"You don't even live around here."

"I do now."

"You don't even have no family."

"I do have a family."

"Not that you live with."

"That's none of your business."

"Well, then don't come butting in if you don't have no responsibility for anything."

"At least I didn't marry my sister. Or brother."

Bea raised the gun. "Get off my property."

"Gladly."

Leland's first cousin, Tim Triplett, Jr., was in the northeast corner of the north pine woods with a bow and arrow. His arrow was a hollow reed with a nail in the end. He shot it into a pine tree, retrieved it, shot again. / Selma Michaels had taken Paul Hilderbrand outside her and Raymond's house and was showing him the ten little streaks down the tin roof, fading to eight, or fading out altogether to reappear again lower down the roof. It was where Raymond fell off the roof and broke his leg. "He was trying to hold on all the way down," said Selma. "He didn't have much fingernails left. I'm real sorry about his leg, but it can't help but be funny when you come out here and look at them ten streaks."

After the chicken shoot, Stephen, standing on his front porch at home, fingering the penny in his pocket, saw Terry and Leland at the top of the muddy bank between Mrs. Odum's and the grocery store. He walked over from his house and watched.

"If you want to ride down," said Terry, "you got to get you a piece of cardboard."

In the kitchen, Stephen asked his mother.

"Who's doing it?" she said.

"Terry and Leland."

"Well, I guess that'll be all right. Just be careful not to get in the road. There's a cardboard box in the garage. Come on, I'll cut you out a piece. We'll get you a big piece."

Stephen stood at the top of the bank and looked down the narrow mud path. He sat on the cardboard, slid himself forward a foot, another foot, and he was off: slow . . . fast, faster. He slid into the road ditch, stood, picked up the cardboard, and headed back up top again. It was Terry's turn, then Leland, then Stephen. When Stephen reached the bottom the second time and started to stand, Terry slammed into him. "You got to get out of the way," Terry said.

"I was fixing to."

Then Leland almost slammed into Stephen.

Back at the top of the bank, Leland said, "It's my turn. That one didn't count because you got in the way."

"It's my turn," said Stephen.

Leland pushed Stephen, and tripped him at the same time. Stephen went sliding down the hill, down the mud path, backward. He hit bottom, stood up. "Why did you do that?" he yelled.

"You little prissy."

"I am not."

"You better not come back up this hill."

The gypsy man, walking by, stopped.

Stephen started along the ditch for home. Leland said, "You better not tell your mama."

"I am, too."

"You better not." Leland started running down the hill at Stephen. Stephen started running toward home. Stephen had a good head start. Leland got up too much steam going down the bank and fell.

In the kitchen, Stephen's mother knelt and looked Stephen in the eyes. "I don't care what he did. Don't you run from him if he pushes you. Next time you tell him to stop and if he don't, you push him back, and then if he does anything else you fight him as hard as you can. Do you understand?"

"Yes ma'am."

"I mean it."

"Yes ma'am."

WHEN THE CRAPE myrtles had lost their color in the near darkness, Alease came out by the garage to empty and burn the trash. Harvey and Stephen were at the store. She was thinking she might just go down there and get Stephen so they could read some or listen to the radio.

June Odum was at her clothesline getting some clothes in. June walked over. "Have you seen that man sitting out there by the fence at the Settle Inn?" she said.

"I don't think so."

"Wears a yellow shirt every day?"

"Oh, yes, I did. I saw him the other morning. I think that's the same one. He was walking down to the blinker light."

"Blake told Urleen he said he was kin to some of the Joneses other side of T.R. Said he called it Traveler's Rest instead of T.R. Course you know some do. But not many. Not natural-born people, anyway. But somehow he knew about Train's mule-truck wreck."

"Which Joneses?"

"I don't know. Wonder why he ain't staying with them?"

"I was wondering the same thing."

FAINT YELLOW

AT ABOUT NOONTIME on Friday, Jack Umstead sat on the bench at Train's Place, drinking a Blatz. Beside him sat Casey Odell, drinking a Tru-Ade orange and eating a honey bun.

"Where did Trouble take his morning nap?" asked Umstead.

"I don't know. You can ask Train. But don't bet no money on whether or not it's going to rain."

Across the road, a woman was approaching the front door of the barbershop. She held a tray of hot lunch under a red-checkered cloth. There was a sign over the door: SHOWER, 25 CENTS.

"I tell you one thing," said Casey, "I hope I can get me a wife that'll bring me a hot lunch every day. She does it every day, too. Ever single day, rain or shine, cold or hot. Yessir."

"Where they live?"

"Top of the hill, back that way, fourth house on the left. She don't ever miss a day neither."

The barbershop was just not a place for hoarding money, thought Umstead. Their house might be.

They sat for a while. A dump truck with a load of gravel came to a long brake-squealing stop at the blinker light.

Umstead said, "I guess the blinker light cut out some accidents."

"Oh, yeah. One of the worst was when this woman pulled out from right over there about time this guy started passing coming from down that way. And I want you to know: It was headlight to headlight. Headlight to headlight. I was under my truck in that pit around there, and it sounded like a atom bomb exploded and if you ever see that woman, Bernice Gallager, she's got a big scar acrost her forehead and walks with a limp. She had a dog in the car that was killed outright and a baby in there, her cousin's baby, didn't get a scratch. The man was from out in Bailford. She's never got over it. Never will.

"Then like I said what made them decide to go ahead and put in the light—the final straw—except it didn't have nothing to do with the intersection directly, was the mule-truck head-on. That's the wreck everybody talks about."

"Does anybody ever go to the picture show down at the school on Friday nights?"

"Oh yeah, they usually have a right good crowd."

Train came rolling out. "Trouble. Sic . . . *sic.*"

Trouble stood with some effort and started his journey around the store.

"Where'd he take his morning nap?" asked Umstead.

"Out here. I bet you two dollars it don't rain today."

"Naw. I been warned about that."

STEPHEN CAME RUNNING across the backyard. Leland was chasing him. Stephen opened the screen door, half fell onto the porch as he turned and hooked the screen door just before Leland grabbed it and pulled.

"You scaredy-cat. You chicken," said Leland, breathing hard. He wiped his nose with the back of his hand.

Stephen turned to go on into the house. But he was face to face with his mama. She grabbed his shoulders, backed him against the porch wall. Her hands were wet. "Don't you run from him again. Ever. Now you get back out there and fight him. You hear me? Get back out there right now and don't you come back in this house until you're finished one way or another. Now get out there." She unhooked the door and pushed him out, hooked it back, and went inside, over to the window to watch. With her apron she wiped dishwater off the back of her hands.

Stephen faced Leland. He saw Leland's fists ball up. He balled up his. Then Leland was right up in his face. Stephen smelled him. He smelled like danger. Stephen's legs were trembling. Leland pushed against Stephen's chest with his fist. Stephen felt a good deal of strength in the push. He put both fists against Leland's chest and pushed. It didn't seem to make a lot of difference somehow. Leland pushed him again, harder, and reached for the Gene Autry pistol at his side. Stephen saw he was about to get hit with it. Leland was swinging it right toward his head. He ducked, the pistol grazed the top of his head. Stephen reached with both hands for Leland's face. He grabbed flesh and squeezed. One hand was knocked loose. He grabbed back, tried to scratch at Leland's eyes. Leland swung the pistol again without Stephen seeing it coming and it hit him upside the head but it didn't hurt at all. It just stopped the hearing on that side. He felt some success. He turned and grabbed the screen door. It was locked. Leland grabbed his shirt. Stephen pulled loose and started to run toward the garage, remembered, stopped, and turned. The thrown pistol hit him in the chest. It didn't hurt a bit. He picked it up and ran several steps toward Leland with the gun over his head, ready to throw. He threw it, missed, but as Leland backed up he tripped. Stephen jumped on top of him, letting his knee drop as hard as he could, felt it sink into Leland's stomach, heard the rush of breath, scratched at Leland's face with his left hand, swung with his right. It was blocked. Leland was giving up, looked like he couldn't breathe. A great rush of energy. Stephen swung hard—his hand got through, made a hard splat sound on Leland's nose. Blood came freely. Stephen stood up, alarmed. Leland rolled over onto his side, finally got his breath, put his hand to his nose, and looked at the blood.

"Leland," said Stephen's mother, through the window, "you go on home now, you hear."

Leland stood up slowly, wiped his nose with his hand, looked at it, at Stephen. "You better not ever come in my yard again."

"We'll see about that," said Stephen's mother. "You shouldn't use that gun. That's not fair. You ought to use your bare hands. Stephen, come on in the house. Now." She unhooked the door for him and in the kitchen she took his milk bottle from warm water on the stove, gave it to him with an asthma pill, and told him to go rest on the couch.

A student from Duke University aimed his camera at a side window of the flintrock store. Peeled paint along with the rust on the bars had caught his eye. / Andrew, over in T.R., had just helped his favorite aunt sell her car because she couldn't see much anymore. As he and his eight-year-old granddaughter pulled into the driveway, the little girl asked, "Will it snow this winter?" and he was trying to answer so that she would not see him crying. / "Some people," said Train to his brother Luke, "will always naturally gravitate to the top and others to the bottom. This is healthy. It gives people something to shoot for. You've got some sense, Luke, if you'd just get off your ass. And do me a favor: Don't try to kill a fly with that blowtorch no more. Use a goddamn flyswatter."

LATE THAT AFTERNOON, around suppertime, Jack Umstead was back, sitting on the bench at Train's Place, drinking a Blatz. Maybe some woman would come walking by going to the picture show at the school. Maybe that Cheryl would go. She was a little bit young, but not too young.

It was almost six-thirty. He couldn't remember if the picture show time was seven or seven-thirty.

A white Cadillac drove up, eased to a stop. Out got a man, reminded him of somebody. The man went inside, came back out with a Coke, sat down on the bench. Umstead looked at the big diamond ring, the Cadillac. Maybe he needn't bother about the Blaine sisters.

"Looks like they gone let MacArthur take care of the Koreans," said the man, staring straight ahead.

"The only good communist is a dead communist," said Umstead. "*That's* who you look like—MacArthur."

"That's what I've been told. More than once . . . Now, if the Russians and the Chinese were to team up we'd be in for a right long haul." The man took a swig of Coke. "Course they ain't got that hydrogen bomb. We *could* just go on and finish it quick. Which is what we should have done done."

Jack Umstead took a swig of beer, crossed his legs. "Does anybody go to the picture show down there at the school on Friday nights?"

"I don't know. I think they do. You're the one living at the Settle Inn, ain't you?"

"Yeah. Staying there while I visit some of my kinfolks."

"Over in T.R.?"

"Pretty good ways on beyond T.R."

"I'm Claude T. Clark."

"Delbert Jones. Pleased to meet you."

"Bunch of gypsies moved in down there at the Settle Inn about a year ago. We finally got some boys to run them out.

You know, they'll steal right out from under your nose—
worse than coons."

"I heard say they wouldn't kill nobody though."

"They got all these irregular beliefs, don't they?" said
Clark, eyeing Umstead.

"I wouldn't be surprised. I hear they're pretty strange.
Strange customs."

"That's right. You belong to a church back where you're
from?"

"Well, yeah, I'm a Baptist back in Mississippi and I'm
thinking about joining the church down there."

"My wife's the secretary down there and damned if she
ain't moved in her office. Sprained her ankle and just decided
to stay over a few days. Got her a little two-eyed hot plate in
there and I don't know what all. She done the same thing last
winter when it snowed."

"Sprained her ankle?"

"Naw, just moved in her office. On account of the snow."

"Seems like I heard about that."

"It's all right with me." Mr. Clark took a swig of Coke.
"But I tell you what. I do miss her. She's a good thing. My first
wife died and I've been mighty lucky on both counts."

"That's a nice car."

"I wouldn't have nothing but a Cadillac."

"I got me a Buick Eight and I'm real pleased with that."

"A Buick's a good car."

Sure enough, at six-thirty, Cheryl Daniels came down her front steps, walked by the barbershop, and kept going toward the school. She walked as if her hips were out in front of her.

"Well, well," said Umstead. "I think I might get on down to the school and watch that movie."

"Take it easy."

"GOING TO THE movie?" Mr. Jones—Delbert—called out as he caught up.

"Yessir."

Cheryl had hoped something exactly like this might happen. He looked just enough like a movie star that she could go ahead and pretend he was.

" 'Yessir?' I thought I told you not to call me that."

"I know."

"How come you ain't working?"

"I get Monday and Friday nights off. And all day Sunday."

"It's a pretty evening, ain't it?"

"It sure is. How old are you, anyway?"

"Thirty-one," he said. "In my prime."

• • •

THAT NIGHT AFTER supper, Stephen's father and mother played policeman with him. He mounted his bicycle with training wheels and wheeled from the kitchen into the dining room, where his father, sitting in a chair, was a policeman holding up his hand for Stephen to stop, then motioning him on into the living room where his mother was the policeman. On each turn he signaled with his arm. A grown-up thing.

Before bed, on the couch in the living room, he listened as his mother read to him from *Aunt Margaret's Bible Stories.*

. . . and while he was building the Ark, people laughed at Noah. They would not believe that anything bad was going to happen. They would not believe in God.

By and by Noah opened the window of the Ark and let out a raven. The raven never came back, because a raven eats dead things, and there were so many dead bodies floating around that it got plenty of food, and never came back to the Ark that had saved it. Noah waited a week, and then he let out a dove, but the dove flew back to the Ark, and Noah took her back and kept her a week, then let her fly again. This time when she came back she brought a sprig of olive branch. Ever since that time the olive branch has meant something good.

Then God made a promise to Noah that no flood should ever drown all the world again, but spring, summer, autumn, and winter, day and night, would go on to the end of the world, when the world would not be drowned by water, but instead be burned up by fire.

Then God gave a gift as a sign of his promise: the rainbow.

AT ABOUT 1:00 A.M., Cheryl flipped back her top sheet. She was fully dressed. She walked very quietly to the front door, opened it, slipped out of the house—it was a warm night—crossed the quiet, silent intersection, and headed toward the Settle Inn. She studied her eerie blinking yellow shadow. She'd done some things, but this was one of the best yet. Delbert Jones might as well be a movie star. She'd kidded him about things. He'd laughed. She'd been hoping for somebody like him to come along since she started reading movie magazines. He was real trustworthy and gentle-like and she was so happy she felt like she could just jump up and down. She skipped a couple of times to hurry up. She could hardly hold back from running, so she skipped along like a little girl.

After the movie, while they had sat by themselves in the dark on the top row of the grandstand, Delbert had told her all about moving away from the other side of T.R. down to Columbia, South Carolina, and then on to Rolling Fork, Mississippi; told her about the grandstand down there in Rolling Fork where he'd played high school baseball and had been scouted by the Boston Red Sox; about the movies they took of him, movies he had in his room back at the Settle Inn along with a projector. Would she mind letting him kiss her right now? he'd asked—he was very polite—and then later on if she could come on down to the Settle Inn, he'd show her the movies of him and maybe they could kiss a little more, go for a late-night ride over to Summerlin, or T.R., or somewhere, ride in his new car with the windows down letting the night air in after such a hot day. Then he could let her off near her house and she could be in bed for a few hours of sleep before morning. A fun little plan.

THAT AFTERNOON MRS. Toomey had taken Stephen with her to cut Bea and Mae Blaine's toenails, and in the night of that day, as Jack Umstead sat beside Cheryl Daniels in the grandstand after watching *The Best Years of Our Lives,* Stephen played with his doodie in a serious way. Stuck there in his head was an image of Miss Bea pulling her black dress apart at the waist, lifting the upper part of the dress so that her ribs, brought to light and life, alive, in a greenish tint, pulled him into a light green then yellow pulsing place of pure feeling in his doodie, a smooth yellow-green yearning feeling like the train's faraway whistle sound in his ears, getting closer and closer, louder and louder.

• • •

MRS. CLARK SAT on her couch over at the church, content, reading her Bible. She was reading about Moses.

And Moses spake unto all the congregation of the children of Israel, saying, This is the thing which the Lord commanded, saying, Take ye from among you an offering unto the Lord; whosoever is of a willing heart, let him bring it, an offering of the Lord; gold, and silver, and brass, and blue, and purple, and scarlet, and fine linen, and goats' hair, and rams' skins dyed red, and badgers' skins, and shittim wood. And oil for the light, and spices for anointing oil, and for the sweet incense, and onyx stones, and stones to be set for the sphod, and for the breastplate.

They were so colorful back then, she thought. She skipped along and read,

And every man, with whom was found blue, and purple, and scarlet, and fine linen, and goats' hair and red skins of rams, and badgers' skins, brought them . . . And all the women that were wise-hearted did spin with their hands, and brought that which they had spun, both of blue, and of purple, and of scarlet, and of fine linen. And all the women whose heart's stirred them up in wisdom spun goats' hair.

And then there was some writing about slaves and the Levites, the ones who got in trouble. It was all so interesting, even though she couldn't quite take in the meaning of it all. It was history! True history!

JUST AFTER THE film *Hot in the Kitchen* started, Delbert stopped the projector. "I'm as sorry as I can be, Cheryl. This ain't what it's supposed to be. I swear I thought . . . I guess I brought the wrong box of films. This here is some sultry stuff my brother left behind when he went to Germany."

"What's 'sultry'?"

"Naked people and such as that. Cavorting around. It's really kind of fun."

"Can we watch it?" He was fun, and smart, and polite, thought Cheryl.

"Well, yeah, if you want to. We'll watch some of it."

Right in the middle of the film, he stopped the projector and told Cheryl his big problem in life: a condition he was ashamed of, and that maybe they could talk about it—did she mind?—and then after he told her as tenderly and meekly as he could that he had a weakness for lying and that he had lied some to her out of embarrassment because of a very unlucky past, and that he had a thinking condition that made him not be able to control some of his thinking and doing. After telling her all that, he asked her if she had anything she was ashamed of. And here she told him she didn't have any big problems in life, nothing that she was ashamed of except her daddy and maybe her mama sometimes—the way they acted some-times.

And later while they talked after they'd made love—making love, he was the most kind and gentle person, and oh, he knew how to wait while he moved his tongue in and out between her fingers and made this sound deep in his throat, making her want to make the same sound—later, she told him that the Settle Inn was where the gypsies always stopped when they came through, but that nobody in Listre would go down there while they were there, and everybody hid things that could be stolen, and that she'd always wanted to come down to the Settle Inn and talk to them and watch them, but she was afraid to tell that to anybody, had never told that to anybody before because everybody said some of the gypsies were witches and that they all had wild habits and would steal you blind.

She saw a faint yellow on his blood-vesseled arms, yellow through a slit in the blinds—on off on off on off—the glow, blinking away seconds of her life, one after another, one less, another less second in which to take all the love she could get from this movie star man before he might have to leave for some reason. She was afraid he might leave, but she wouldn't say that.

He said that there were lots of things he could tell her, and that she could pretend he was a gypsy if she wanted to. A good one. He had even traveled with a bunch of gypsies between Carrollton, Georgia, and New Orleans when he was selling knives one time.

He whispered to her, "I love you." He kept his lips on her ear after he said it.

"I love you, too. I love you like mad. Is there anything you ain't done?"

"A few things. I ain't ever throwed up from drinking and I ain't ever hit a woman. I even had a small part in a movie one time. Probably not one you would have heard about. It was called *The Wild Idiot* and it starred some unknowns."

"Was it sultry?"

"Oh, no. I wouldn't do that."

SHOVEL PRINTS

JACK UMSTEAD WAS back in his chair outside cabin 6, watching the morning traffic, when he heard the car brake, the thump, and the cat's guttural shriek. He looked through the fence: The kitten was by no means dead, but by no means fully alive either. The car kept going——a light blue car.

I could of told you, he said to himself.

How many other black kittens had gotten run over by blue cars that same morning? he wondered. In North Carolina. In Georgia. How many states had that happened in yesterday? Say over ten times. With a blue car. What percentage of all cats would die in ten years from automobiles? As up against poisoning——accidental poisoning. As up against intentional poisoning. He couldn't remember ever hearing about a cat getting accidentally poisoned. So intentional would be higher. Something like 3 percent intentional to 0 percent accidental, and something like 20 percent death by automobile. Of . . . well, no . . . it was more dogs it seemed like on death by automobile. A few more anyway. Maybe not that many more.

The kitten had been knocked into the Toomey yard and was flopping and flipping around. One of the two boys on the porch—the Toomey boy—was running toward it. Ten feet or so from the kitty he stopped and watched it flip and flop. One of its eyeballs was hanging out.

The boy screamed and cried, "Inky, Inky, Mama, Mama," then ran into the house, leaving the other boy walking out toward the cat, kind of tiptoeing in the grass.

Maybe he ought to go on over and kill it.

Flip . . . flip . . . flop-flip.

The Toomey woman ran down the front porch steps, around the house toward the garage out back. "Stephen, stay on the porch," she called.

The boy stood on the edge of the porch, crying, his arms buried between his legs, his face red and contorted. Mrs. Toomey came running with the ax, heaved it up over her head. She heaved it up too far, stepped backward a step, off balance. "Lord, his eyeball is out," she said. "Move back, Terry." She swung downward. The ax blade buried itself short of the kitten.

On the next swing she was well balanced and didn't heave the ax so far back behind her head. In fact, she didn't lift it very high at all, but on its downward fall, the kitten flopped out of the way and the ax was buried in the ground again.

"Terry," said the Toomey woman, "you think you can kind of hold that cat down with your foot? I'll be careful."

"No ma'am."

Umstead saw the drunk man who lived there, hair sticking out in every direction, come out onto the porch steps barefoot, stand, gather in what seemed to be happening, then say something—ask the boy a question.

"He got run over," the boy wailed.

Umstead realized the man had said, "What the hell did that kitty *do?*"

JUNE ODUM, WONDERING what in Lord's name, walked over from her yard, across the driveway, an unlit Pall Mall hanging from her lips. She stopped a few yards from the kitten, lit her Pall Mall with her flip-top lighter out of her apron pocket, her eyes on the kitten as the ax cleanly separated its head and body. At the cat's mouth, a slight grin appeared and disappeared. A body shiver, then both parts rested still. She squinted, removed the cigarette from her mouth, looked at the remains. "You just can't beat a cat for a pet, can you?" she said.

"I hate cats," said Terry. "But that one was a good one."

FOR STEPHEN, THE kitten, no longer moving at all, rested at the center of all space and all objects and at the end of all time. It had belonged to him. It was his own. Now it was just plain dead. It couldn't move.

He sat down on the porch steps, Terry sat down on the grass, his mother rested the ax on the ground—her hand on the handle as if it were a cane.

Mr. Jones, the gypsy man, walked up. "That's a shame about that kitty," he said.

ALEASE FELT A satisfaction that came from doing the right thing when the right thing was hard to do and when a lot of other people would have been unable to do it. She'd taken things into her own hands and solved the problem. Her mother had been that way, and her grandmother. Without her to finish it up, there's no telling what would have happened. "It is a shame," she said, "but somebody had to put him out of his misery."

STEPHEN WALKED OUT into the yard from the porch steps and wailed another long, desperate cry. His mother, holding the ax, walked to him and put her arm around his shoulder. Stephen screamed straight up into the sky, "I'm going to kill them. They run over Inky. They was in a blue car."

"It *was* a blue car, Budrow," said the gypsy man.

Stephen dropped to his knees out of his mother's grasp, looked up at the gypsy man. There was a picture in his head of the inside of the world, a moving picture of the inside of the world going around and around like water spinning inside a bucket so fast it was climbing the bucket walls and the colors were a green and yellow and brown. He looked up at his mother. "Why did you have to do that?"

"Honey, there are some things you can't help and he had to be put out of his misery. And whoever it was didn't mean to run over him. It's no need to get mad at them. And you shouldn't ever say you're going to kill somebody."

"They didn't even slow down."

"Well," said the gypsy man, "they did touch the brake before they hit him."

"It was just all in all bad timing," said Mrs. Odum. "You just can't tell what a car is liable to hit," she said. "My uncle Searcy had a cow hit by one one time," she kept on. "He got over s'emty steaks out of it."

Stephen said to his mother, "Why did *you* have to do it— have to *kill* him?" He started crying again.

"I was the only one could."

UMSTEAD DECIDED HE wanted to be a little more involved. "You got a brave mama, son. Ain't many women'll do something like that. You got a shovel, ma'am? I'll bury that kitty for you."

"You're the one kin to some of the Joneses over in T.R.?" said the neighbor woman.

"Yes'um. Beyond T.R. a ways. My name's Delbert Jones. And you're . . ."

"June Odum." That's a Pall Mall she's smoking.

"Alease Toomey." Deep red in her hair.

"Raleigh Caldwell." Drunk. Crazy hair.

"Pleased to meet y'all. I saw you feeding your boy the other morning, Mrs. Toomey."

"Oh, yes."

"Urleen, Blake's wife, told me about you," said Mrs. Odum. "Blake, down at Train's Place."

"I know Blake and them boys. Yeah, my folks moved off not too long after I was born. Moved down to Columbia, South Carolina, and then after a few years there, we moved to Mississippi."

"Which Joneses was 'at?"

"There was a Annie Jones I guess was the main one." Get off it. "You got a shovel, ma'am?" he said to Mrs. Toomey. "I'll bury that kitty for you."

"There was a Annie Jones over in Bethel. You not talking about the Annie Jones from over in Bethel are you?"

"No'um. Not in Bethel, I don't think. My people stayed mostly to theirselves. And they weren't here all that long either. Back over beyond T.R. You got a shovel, Mrs. Toomey? I'll just take this little kitty across the road and bury him."

"Well, yes, we got a shovel in the smokehouse. But . . . Stephen, go get the shovel."

"We used to have a sawdust pile where we buried all our animals," Umstead said, "and we had a worship service every time. I'll take care of it."

"Can I go?" said the neighbor boy.

"How about just burying him out in the field behind the house," said the boy's mama. "I don't want Stephen crossing that road," she said. "And we buried two goldfish out there. Just beyond that middle tree. And you'll do a little service?"

"Yes'um."

He thought her eyes were a little steadier on his than they needed to be.

"You can go with them, Terry," the Toomey woman said. "Then you need to be running on home, son. I think I'll just sit on the porch for a minute."

Umstead, with the shovel holding the two pieces of Inky and bits of grass, headed for the field behind the house. The two boys followed him. At the edge of the field—field peas it looked like—just beyond the middle tree he placed the kitten on the ground. He couldn't quite get over the small size of North Carolina fields. In the Delta a field could be well over a thousand square acres. In the Carolinas they were sometimes littler than a bed. He looked across the way to the back of Pendergrass Grill. Cheryl might come out to throw something away. Then he looked at the Toomey garage. "Let's go on over closer to the garage where your mama's got some flowers started." He scooped the kitty up into the shovel. "A kitty ought to make right good fertilizer for some flowers." Near the back corner of the garage he dug a hole about the size of a water bucket. Skimpy layer of topsoil, he thought. With the point of the shovel he raked the head and body into the hole, then raked in all the loose dirt and smacked it twice, leaving shovel prints.

Raleigh, the drunk, walked up pretty unsteady. "I could have done this."

"There's more dirt in there than they was before," said Terry.

"I could of done this," said Raleigh.

"I don't mind."

"Where'd the extra dirt come from?" asked Terry.

"What's that, Budrow?"

"Where'd that extra dirt come from?"

"There's a kitten in there now. Before there won't. He's taking up space. Shall we all bow our heads for a moment of prayer? For God so loved the world He gave His only begotten son that whosoever believeth in Him should not perish but have everlasting life. Amen. Now. Son, you want to say a word about your cat?"

"Sir?"

"Your cat. You want to say something?"

"No sir."

"I don't think he knows what you're talking about," said Raleigh. "Say something good about the cat, boy."

"He chased balls," said Terry.

"Well, hell, I know that. Stephen needs to say something religious, for Christ's sake. It was his cat—but his mama was the one taking care of it. Say something."

Pall Mall walked up. "Did y'all say a prayer?"

"Yes ma'am, we did," said Umstead. "And we're doing some more right now."

"I don't think I know any animal prayers, except I don't guess there's no reason to make a animal prayer any different from a human prayer. After all, humans are animals too, or so say the dern science books."

"Do cats go to heaven?" Stephen asked.

"Better ask your uncle that one," said Umstead.

"Do they?" he asked his uncle.

"Why, hell no. They never accepted Jesus, have they?"

"I don't know."

"Why, hell no. They go to Ratland where there's rats as big as tigers. That's where things get evened up."

"Once she got the bead on him," said Umstead, "she popped him a pretty clean cut."

"I always heard that good animals go to heaven," said Mrs. Odum.

The mother, Alease, walked up.

"Mama," said Stephen, "I think I'm getting asthma."

"Let's go inside and get you a pill, then. Terry, it's time for you to go on home, son."

Raleigh reached for the shovel, took it, staggered, and said to Umstead, "Kids nowadays don't know the first damn thing about work. That boy ain't seen a hour's work in his life and he's almost s'em years old." He added a few pats to the little grave.

They all started toward the Toomey house.

"You in the war?" Umstead asked.

"The Great War."

"You don't look that old." Umstead thought he looked like he might have fought in the War Between the States.

"I'll be fifty-seven twenty-third of December."

"Yeah, well . . . I saw a little time in the Second World War. I got in right at the end. I was lucky, I guess."

"Looks like there's gonna be another one."

"Yeah, I'd say there is. How'd you lose your arm?"

"Shrapnel. Hindenburg line. October 1918."

"That's a shame."

Umstead wondered how many arms and legs were lost in the two big wars. How many lefts and how many rights. He figured it was probably more rights. Just the nature of things. "Did you hear the story about the soldier got shot in the leg and his buddy took him to the medic tent?" Umstead asked Raleigh.

"I don't think so."

"Soldier got shot in the leg. 'My leg, my leg!' he hollered. His buddy picked him up and throwed him over his shoulder like a sack of feed and started running toward the medic tent. About that time, a stray cannonball shot the hurt soldier's head off and the buddy didn't know it. At the medic's tent the buddy threw the soldier up on the operating table and the medic said, 'Why'd you bring *him* in? His *head* is shot off.' And the buddy said, "Well, hell—he told me it was his *leg*."

"Yeah, I heard that one."

The two boys caught up. Raleigh said to Stephen, "That cat wouldn't be dead had you took care of him right. There is certain things you got to do when you're taking care of a ani-mal. If you'd paid attention to what I told you he wouldn't have to be out there dead and buried."

"Mama's been taking care of him."

Jack Umstead lingered as Raleigh and the boys walked ahead. He had a chance to speak to Alease for a few minutes. "There's a kind of satisfaction to just doing something right, ain't there?" he said to her.

ALEASE REALIZED THAT Harvey, because of how he was, his whole being and history, would never think to say that. "There was nobody else to do it," she said.

"Anything suffering like that needs to be put out of their misery," said Mr. Jones. "Reminds me about the electric chair. Some people suffer a lot longer in that thing than they tell you about. I don't know why they don't just gas everybody. I'd rather have my head cut off than be electrocuted. I've got shocked before doing various things. One time when I was working on electric lines — on a telephone pole. It's a jolting experience."

"'Jolting?'" Alease frowned and smiled together.

"That's the word: jolting."

"I took Stephen up to see the electric chair — to show him what can happen."

"If he don't be good, you mean."

"That's right." Alease brushed hair back from her eye. He seemed to understand. "I took both them boys."

"Sounds like a pretty good idea to me. When I was in grammar school in Mississippi they had a portable electric chair they'd take around and show. I never knew anybody that saw that thing to get in trouble. By the way, I buried the kitty next to the garage instead of behind that middle tree. I noticed you'd started some flowers out there and a little animal like that'll be useful fertilizer."

She stopped and looked toward the garage. Harvey hadn't got the poles yet. "I'm trying to get a flower bed started out there, but with Raleigh and all I just haven't had time to get it going."

"I'd be happy to do some digging for you. I'm looking for something to keep me busy. I got a few days before I head on back home."

"You've seen your relatives?" He was a handsome man, she thought. In his own way.

"Yeah, and it . . . it just didn't turn out exactly like I'd hoped it would. It's just a sad story."

"Well . . ."

"You think about it—me helping you out a little bit—and let me know. I wouldn't charge you nothing."

"That's mighty nice of you. Stephen, son, let's go on and take you a pill. Go ahead to the house, son."

AT THE GRILL, Umstead could tell that Cheryl was crazy to see him. And he'd had such a good time with her that he was right glad to see her, but this Alease presented a whole new kind of interest to him. She was mature and strong. And married.

"Hey, Cheryl. How you this morning?" He sat at his place.

"I'm a little bit sleepy. You want the usual?"

"I always want the usual."

Cheryl leaned onto the counter. "I been thinking all morning about how that blinker light came in through the shades and lit up your arm. Kind of blink . . . blink . . . blink."

"I been thinking a little myself. Let me have a couple of them biscuits, too. And some strawberry jelly, if you got it. I don't see nothing here but grape."

DIRTY ENERGY

NEXT MORNING, RALEIGH eased down the front steps and on across the yard toward the Jones fellow sitting out in his chair. Jones might be able to offer him some relief.

"Morning."

"Morning."

"So you're just passing through?" said Raleigh.

"Yeah, more or less. Visiting some kinfolks. But it's hard to stay in the house with them. Have a seat there. They're just a little too hard to stay with."

Raleigh kept standing. "Oh, man. I tell you. It's a right pretty morning."

"Sure is." Jones shaded his eyes from the morning sun.

"I was just wondering. I couldn't buy a little drink off you, could I? In case you might have one."

"Well, I keep a bottle in the trunk of my car there. Trunk should be open."

"Oh, that'd be nice." Raleigh headed for the trunk. "I'll be glad to pay you—I'm sort of coming down off a little spell and my sister's got my bottle. I just had a taxi bring me one and damn if she didn't get it. I told the son of a bitch to stop next door, and damned if he didn't drive right up in the yard and blow the damn horn. I'll be glad to pay you." He reached into the bag.

"Don't worry about that. There's some little paper cups in the bag."

"Yeah, right here. You got something a little bigger by any chance? Oh shit, there she comes. Never mind." Now she was messing it all up again.

The Jones man stood.

Raleigh said to Alease, "I said I was stepping outside for a minute."

"I want you back in the house, now. You need to get in the house and eat some breakfast. Come on. Your breakfast is ready. I didn't know where you were."

"I told you I was stepping outside." She *should* have heard.

"Well, you didn't say it so I could hear you."

"I did, too."

Raleigh headed back toward the house, the damn house.

UMSTEAD NOTICED THAT Alease hesitated, just the briefest second. "Have you thought anymore about me doing a little work for you?"

"Well, I don't know. I hate not to pay you but we don't usually pay for yard work. I try to do all my own yard work, except sometimes it seems like I don't have much time."

"I did rethink my offer. I am going to need some pay."

"Oh? . . . Well, I—"

"I haven't had a real good glass of iced tea in a long time."

STEPHEN WENT OUT on the porch looking for his mama. The gypsy man over there was talking to her. That man could dig big shovels full of dirt every time. Uncle Raleigh was walking toward the house, looking down at the ground. The gypsy man stepped back a step and laughed. His mother stepped back too, and then turned to look at him standing there on the porch. She had a big laugh on her face. Then she looked like she remembered something.

Stephen wanted her to come on back and play the breakfast game. He was hungry. "Mama, I'm hungry."

DOWN AT THE church, as Mrs. Clark thought about Jesus being right there last night for a second night that week, a pain shot through her ankle. She was sitting on the couch and had put just a little weight on it. She reached over, got her pills and capsules, a couple extra for the pain, took them with a cup of water, and lay back down.

So it was all true. Everything about God and Jesus was true. She'd had the whole thing revealed to her right there outside her office door. There was, after all, a reason she had sprained her ankle——the reason was so she could meet Jesus face to face. As good as face to face.

She prayed her morning prayer, felt close to the Lord. Somebody was coming up the stairs. Good. Could it be . . . ? No, that was the preacher's sound. She could always tell the preacher's sound.

PREACHER CRENSHAW NOTICED a new poster on the stair wall——announcing the youth trip to Lake Blanca. He had to write a letter to Cheryl Daniels. Immediately. She'd called him on the phone at home the night before to be sure he could carry four or five boys in his car and they got to talking and talked and talked and he'd laughed and kidded her about a very thin tomato slice she'd served him on a hamburger at the grill.

This durn tornado had come along winding right on into his life, a life in God's service, going along so smoothly: he had his own church, his own congregation, his own choir, choir director, his own precious and sincere relationship to

Jesus and God, his own house and expense account, discretionary fund, his own five well-behaved children, his own faithful, hardworking wife, and his own secretary. And now winding and tearing its way into his life was this warm red tornado—way younger than him for heaven's sake—no matter how hard he kept trying to close the door to it. This tornado, just a little tornado at first, but it grew every time he saw her. There were more sparks and life and fireworks in her eyes than he could bear to *look* at, and she must have a body underneath there like nothing he'd ever even been able to imagine, and now she was in charge of taking a youth group to Lake Blanca next Saturday morning and had asked him to come along—to drive a carload of kids. Her real motive, he knew, was so they could be *together*—he just knew that had to be her real motive—and he'd awakened at 3:11 A.M., looked at the lighted tips on the clock hands, and said to himself that he shouldn't go to Lake Blanca . . . then . . . then he thought that he *had* to go to Lake Blanca for the good of the youth, the church. They did need another driver. But maybe that's not why he was going really. Then he couldn't go back to sleep because he knew good and well he needed to talk to God about this. He hadn't talked to God about it because he wanted to handle it himself. It wasn't exactly the kind of thing he wanted to bring God in on unless it got real bad.

Well, it was real bad, and so he had prayed. And prayed, and prayed.

He'd not felt an answer from God in the middle of the night, but he'd expected one the next morning. During breakfast while the kids were sleeping and Marjorie was drinking coffee and reading the newspaper — she used way too much sugar in her coffee — during breakfast he felt God speak to him, and God said write Cheryl Daniels a letter. Cheryl was a full-fledged woman and he had to go ahead and treat her like one, head off this business at the pass. Go ahead. Get on over there to the office and sit down and write Cheryl Daniels a business letter, spelling out things — as a man of God. The way he had to be. A business letter would get her attention, would finish all this off for good. God was there for him, providing an answer to prayer, so he headed over to the church to write that letter.

Going up the steps inside the church he thought about what to write. "Dear Cheryl." "Dear Cheryl Daniels, it's always a joy to see you at church." "Dear Cheryl." "My dearest Cheryl." "Dear Cheryl, let's get right down to business."

The warm tornado was not only full of sex, that word, full of an animal body pull somehow, not only that — Cheryl Daniels *made fun* of him in the best way in the world, just like they were old buddies. "Preacher Crenshaw, you're going to have a *heart attack* you don't ease up up there while you're preaching. You got to learn to relax and have some fun." It was almost totally clear that she was talking about some kind of fooling around. "Preacher Crenshaw, the only reason I'm going back for seconds is I *know* you're going back for thirds and I don't want you to feel bad." She could just *reach out* to him with her eyes, somehow. "Preacher Crenshaw, you need a haircut." Her whole attitude was fun fun fun fun fun fun fun. Some kind of control was missing.

> *Dear Cheryl,*
>> *I believe that we need to think about*

He crumpled the paper and threw it into the trash can.

> *Dear Cheryl,*
>> *I must say that I find you attractive in a way that*

Trash can again. There were other things he needed to be doing. Mrs. Blount had called three times in the last three days asking him to come see her. He hadn't been up to the hospital in . . . what, four days?

> *Dear Cheryl,*
>> *I have fallen deeply in love with you. This is a simple truth. I'm sorry to say it but I have. I know I will be sorry for*

writing this to you but my heart has been captured beyond my earthly control. I wish I could keep from writing you this letter. Sometimes I imagine us together alone. Sometimes I imagine that your eyes are so close to mine that our noses must gently touch, and then our lips, moist and quivering. I want to take care of you in every way you can be taken care of. Would but that I could be that close to you if for no more than thirty minutes in this feeble, sinful life of mine. I want to touch you, taste you, hold your beating heart to mine.

He pushed the paper aside, put his head down on his wrists. He was going to need every ounce of clean physical strength in his body to fight this sin. And in order to write this letter he might have to first rid himself of the dirty animal energy rising up in him. He couldn't go home and do it right now because the kids were just getting up, but if he didn't do something quick then he was going to end up writing an awful letter. He would have to commit a short-lasting sin—in order to stop a big, long-lasting one.

MRS. CLARK WAS so glad she was in the Lord's house. The Lord's house was safe. The preacher, God's messenger, was now in his place. Things were in order. She had heard the preacher slide his desk chair back. Then after a goodly pause, she heard him leave. She heard the bathroom door open and close. Maybe if she didn't put much weight on her foot. She tried to stand. Yes. There was a way she could sort of put weight on the heel of her foot and the cane at the same time so as to avoid that sharp pain. He might have written a letter for her to type, or some notes for the bulletin.

IN THE BATHROOM, Crenshaw sat on the commode. There was a faint lingering person smell. Was that himself? He put his face in his hands. He'd have to go back in there and finish that letter so that . . . "Dear God," he said. "Oh, dear God." This was a crisis. This was a visit from the Devil himself, and . . . That's it! God was calling him to preach a sermon on temptation.

MRS. CLARK APPROACHED Preacher Crenshaw's desk, walking haltingly with her cane. She saw that he *had* written a letter. Well, good. She dropped a wad of warm Kleenexes from his desk into the trash can, picked up the letter, read it, placed it back on his desk, and hurried as best she could back to her office. This was very, very troubling. This was a crisis. Did all this have something to do with Jesus being around, Himself?

Just after sunset, Bud Thornton moved the droplight from behind the carburetor to in front of it.

He'd dropped his wrench and it hadn't made it all the way to the ground. Lilly, his wife, called him in to supper. He was hungry. He'd find the wrench later, when he came back out. And when he did come back out, his hunger relieved, the night air cooling the hot day, the evening sky not yet black, all that together would sit pleasantly on his work. / Train, down at Train's Place, was talking to Luke: "Listen, Luke, there's more for you to do around here than sit on your ass on that drank crate. I've said it before and I'll say it again: It takes more than a performer to keep a traveling show on the road. Who's gone put up the goddamn tent? Now, go on out there and stack them tires like I told you yesterday."

AN ACCIDENT

NOONTIME ON SATURDAY, Jack Umstead sat alone on the bench at Train's Place, drinking a Blatz. He was thinking he might have to get Mrs. Clark to get that letter she told him about so he could take a picture of it, mail it in to the preacher, asking for some kind of big money payment. He could certainly believe that the preacher meant his own Cheryl right there across the road.

Blake Redding came out and sat down on the bench with him.

Trouble yawned.

"Do you know anybody else named Cheryl Daniels?" he asked Blake.

"Girl lives over there. Johnny Daniels's daughter."

"Anybody else?"

"Her mama. She's both their — she's the daughter of both of them."

"I mean you know anybody else named Cheryl Daniels?"

"Oh. I thought you meant was she anybody else's daughter." Blake bent over and started tying his shoe.

"*Do* you know anybody else named Cheryl Daniels?"

"Nope."

BEHIND THE PENDERGRASS Auto Shop, Leland and Terry were digging for fishing worms with a hoe. Stephen stood by, watching.

The hoe blade was sharpened until it shined — sharp as a razor. *Swish-chunk* — Leland hoed up a clump of black dirt. Terry picked it up and shook it, checked it for worms. These boys were doing something very hard to do, something that took planning that was beyond Stephen. They were digging up fishing worms. Then they would walk all the way to the church pond by themselves — and go fishing. Stephen was unable to imagine himself in such a free life.

Leland and Terry were working well together — hoe up dirt, shake the dirt, can the worm, hoe up dirt, no worm, hoe up dirt, no worm, hoe up dirt, can the worm, hoe up dirt — when a *half*-worm dropped and landed wriggling. Terry reached for it just as the hoe commenced its powerful arc downward, razor edge glinting in the sun, the blade cutting down so fast it made a *swish* sound, a sound like a burning rag pulled through the air. *Chunk.* Terry drew his hand back as if he'd touched fire, stopped his hand in midair. The thumb swung back and forth, dangling—a greatly enlarged worm, bunched into a little sausage, running blood all over itself. A bloodworm.

Terry's scream, threaded with something wild, bounced off the tin back of the auto repair shop as he ran toward his house, toward his mama and daddy.

IT WAS A Saturday, the day Johnny Daniels was home drinking because it was by God the end of the week and he deserved a little relaxation and relief from his business of bringing in money to support a wife and daughter and a boy who got on his nerves awful bad sometimes because he couldn't learn things as quick as—my God Almighty, what the hell was that god-awful screaming about? *Got*-damn. Somebody— it was Terry—was into wasps or got bit by something, something still holding on. Wasps, probably.

STEPHEN AND LELAND—both walking—followed Terry, who, holding his thumb to his shirt, disappeared around the back corner of the auto shop. Stephen looked at the hoe propped on Leland's shoulder—like a soldier carries a rifle. Leland stopped, held out the hoe, dropped it. "I gotta go get a drink of water," he said.

Stephen wondered if maybe *he* had to go get a drink of water, too. But the chopped thumb pulled him toward the Daniels's house and when he rounded the corner, he saw Mr. Daniels cross the road, walk kind of wobbly to meet Terry, ask him something, and before Terry could answer, hit him with his open hand in the butt hard enough to propel Terry forward toward their house. Terry had placed the thumb back and was holding it there. Maybe it would stick back and hold. Maybe the blood would work like glue and fasten the thumb back the way it had been—with nothing to show but a thin red line.

Terry went straight inside, probably to tell his mother sitting in her big chair in the dark living room. She was probably sewing something and listening to the radio, her eyes squinting in her cigarette smoke.

Stephen thought about Terry, the way he was, always kind of back inside himself, as if looking out from inside something, maybe like a rabbit looking from inside a rabbit box, afraid to come out, not like Leland at all, Leland who went ahead and did whatever he wanted to do to whoever he wanted to do it to, no matter what. Then Stephen heard, inside the house, Mr. Daniels holler and Mrs. Daniels scream. And in a sweat, in a heat suddenly covering his head and ears, Stephen almost became Terry afraid inside his own house, and he wanted somebody to go in there and get him out and take him to the hospital. He started home, to tell his mother.

Somebody called loud from the bench over at Train's Place: "What happened?" It was Mr. Blake. Mr. Blake and the gypsy man had stood up from the bench.

"Terry cut his thumb just about off. It's hanging by a little piece of skin."

They crossed the road, walked up the steps, and knocked on the Daniels's door. Stephen looked both ways like his mama had taught him, then followed them. He felt like the two men might be able to do a good job of making everything all right. They were happy beer drinkers. They could take Terry to the hospital, where they might could fix it back.

Then Cheryl rode up on her bicycle, leaned it against the steps, said something to the gypsy man, and hurried into the house.

In a few minutes, Mr. Blake drove his black car into the narrow front yard while Stephen and other bystanders watched. The Daniels family appeared and started down the steps, pretty high steps, except for Cheryl, who stood back in the doorway. Terry had stopped crying and his right hand was wrapped in a bloody pillowcase. He looked whiter, and a little more yellow, than he usually did.

From across the road came Leland—led by the elbow by Mrs. Pendergrass.

Mr. Daniels was holding Terry's elbow as they started down the high front-porch steps. Mr. Daniels saw Leland, stopped, lost his balance, caught it. "What happened, Leland?" he said.

"I didn't do nothing," said Leland. And then he pointed. "Stephen done it," he said.

Heads turned. The gypsy man, closest to Stephen, stepped back to give the world room enough to look on him, and then the attention of all the people swung back to Terry, up on the steps.

Terry raised his unwrapped hand and pointed. "Stephen done it," he said.

Stephen turned, looked both ways, ran across the road and behind Train's Place, where he had never been before, and on toward home. He looked down at the road shoulder, rocks, dirt, and grass flying under him, his chest tightening, and finally, in the kitchen, he told his mother what had happened, all of it, as fast as he could, crying, trying to get his breath.

"Come in here with me," she said.

He followed her to the bathroom, where she opened the medicine cabinet and got out the bottle of asthma pills, shook one out, and gave it to him with water from the flowered glass that stayed in the bathroom, then led him to the front door, knelt down, put her hands on his shoulders, and told him that there were times in life when you had to do the right thing, no matter what. He had to go back down there by himself, to look both ways when he crossed the road, and tell those people the truth. All those people. Jesus would go with him. She stood and pushed him on out the door.

In the yard, he stopped walking, sat down on the ground, and started crying. His mother walked out to him, knelt down again, helped him up, placed her hands on his shoulders. "You got to do the right thing," she said. "You can't let people tell a story about you and you not do nothing. Jesus'll be with you. And God, too. Now go on like I told you. This is what Jesus and God is for. Look both ways before you cross the road."

Stephen felt as if he were walking toward a firestorm. And then he saw an empty Daniels's porch and yard except for Cheryl sitting on the steps and the gypsy man standing there talking to her. Good. He would tell *them* the truth. That wouldn't be hard.

The gypsy man stood with his back to Stephen, and Cheryl was sitting on the top step with her arms wrapped around her bent knees. As Stephen walked up, the gypsy man turned to leave, then knelt with his hands on his knees, looked Stephen in the face. "What you want, Budrow?"

"Mama told me to come down here and tell the truth."

"Well, what's the truth?"

"I didn't do it."

"You didn't?"

"No sir."

"Well, who you going to tell?"

"You and Cheryl."

"It's okay," said Cheryl. "Come on over here and sit down for a minute, Stephen. Me and Mr. Jones was just talking about things."

"I think I'll amble on back over to Train's Place," said the gypsy man. "I'm getting a little thirsty."

On the steps, Cheryl listened to Stephen, to his story, and then said, "I knew you didn't do it. Let's see if we can find a four-leaf clover for Terry. If we find one maybe they can save his thumb." The way she rose and then settled in a patch of green clover by the steps seemed to Stephen almost as smooth as an angel.

Stephen sat facing her. They talked about the difference between a boy's and girl's bicycle, and then just after Cheryl found a big four-leaf clover she told Stephen that before the

Americans dropped the atomic bomb on Japan, they called up the Japanese and warned them so that the Japanese could get all the little children out of town. She said America had a telephone wire that ran all the way under the Pacific Ocean.

He wondered what "Pacific" meant.

"Now some day when you grow up," said Cheryl, "you'll fall in love like me and you and your sweetheart will look for four-leaf clovers together."

"There's just one girl for me."

"That's right. And I'll tell you a secret if you won't tell anybody. You promise not to tell anybody—not even your mama?"

"Yes ma'am." Stephen felt the color from the asthma pill spreading through his blood.

"I found that person for me. He's that man right over there in the yellow shirt. Delbert. He's the man of my life and we're going to get married and he's going to take me to New York City. I'm the luckiest girl in the world. I hope you find somebody just like I have, but don't you tell anybody now. It'll happen to you someday too, and I hope you're as lucky as I am. But if you tell anybody my mama and daddy would get real real mad and there ain't no telling what they would do."

"Does your daddy ever hit your mama sometimes?"

"Yes." Cheryl spread the clover, looking. "But he buys her

pretty things, too. And he's got a job now. Now, do you promise you won't tell what I just told you about me and Delbert?"

"Yes ma'am."

"You don't have to say 'ma'am' to me, Stephen. And listen. He's the most gentle and the most experienced person I've ever met. He knows so much about the world."

THAT NIGHT, STEPHEN listened as his mother read from *Aunt Margaret's Bible Stories:*

But God pitied Adam and Eve, and us too, and He promised them that the Seed—that is, the Son—of the woman should bruise the serpent's head, and set them and their children free. Our Blessed Lord Jesus Christ, the Son of God, set us free when He died on the cross and then rose again and now we belong to Him, and not to the Devil. Only we must try and ask Him to help us not to do wrong like Eve did, or we shall die from the power of the enemy.

PART 3

Just as I Am

SALVATION

BY LATE WEDNESDAY afternoon, Mrs. Clark had typed the church bulletin, filed several committee reports, rested, and read from her Bible—Psalms. At suppertime she ate a ham sandwich brought over by Mrs. Weams, drank a cup of tomato juice, took her two capsules and the brown pills, and freshened up in the bathroom before people started coming to prayer meeting about a half-hour early, at around seven.

In the sanctuary, Stephen sat on the third pew, inside seat, where he leaned his head into the corner made by the meeting of the seat back and the end of the pew. Soon the hymns would bounce off the wood in that corner, ringing with hard sounds from a place where angels sang. His mama sat beside him. She was dressed for prayer meeting—the same as for church. His father sat in the church foyer with the ushers, though he hardly ever ushered. The ushers wore coats and ties, except sometimes on a Wednesday night one or two wore a shirt without a tie. But the collar would be buttoned.

The ushers handed out bulletins and took up offering in wooden plates with soft fuzzy bottoms. Sometimes he got to drop in a nickel or a dime. At offering time, four of them marched down the middle aisle, two and two, and picked up offering plates from a table. Then while Mrs. Tyndall played songs on the piano, they took up offering, moving from front to back, one along each wall and two up the middle aisle. But Stephen's daddy usually just sat back where you came in. He took up offering once or twice a year — Mr. Jaywright and Mr. Simpson took it up just about every Sunday — but Stephen looked for his daddy anyway. The word "usher" had a kind of magic to it.

FOR HARVEY, THERE was something embarrassingly emotional displayed by preachers, something that made him ashamed of most any sermon he heard. But he could no more stay away from church than he could stay away from food. If he didn't come to church he would get talked about and his mama and papa would hear about it and would want to know why he was forgetting God, and that would be one of the worst possible things that could happen to them. His mama and papa's pew was fifth row, left side. One of their shames was that their youngest, Steve, didn't come to church anymore. As a little boy, he'd sung solos in church. They didn't know what had happened. His papa had said something to Steve about it, but that hadn't made any difference yet.

MRS. CLARK HOBBLED into the auditorium. She'd gotten word from Clara Stott on the phone that Seth Templeton and "some more people" were upset about her staying in the church for a few days. She'd decided her nervousness also had something to do with this awful thing about the preacher and the Daniels girl all mixed in with her talks with Jesus Himself who had come maybe to straighten all that out. All these events had come together, connected, but Jesus had wanted it to be private so she'd better not tell.

She did have to admit that she was about ready to get on back home.

She felt a touch on her shoulder. Jordan Sellers escorted her to her seat. She showed him her ankle. She had used two ankle wraps instead of one so that the swelling would be clearly visible.

JACK UMSTEAD CAME in quietly and sat down on the back row. He was getting to know his way around. He was trying to remember that joke about the fiddle player. What was it? This fiddle player . . . Oh yes. This fiddle player plays a solo in church. It's awful. Sounds like a cat dying. Somebody says out loud, "The fiddle player is a son of a bitch." "Who said that?" says the preacher, standing up, looking. Silence. The preacher continues, "Who was sitting beside whoever said the fiddle player was a son of a bitch?" Silence. "Who was sitting beside whoever was sitting beside whoever said the fiddle player was a son of a bitch?" Silence. A man stands up. "Preacher, I didn't say the fiddle player was a son of a bitch, and I ain't sitting beside whoever said the fiddle player was a son of a bitch, and I ain't sitting beside whoever was sitting beside whoever said the fiddle player was a son of a bitch. But what I want to know is this: Who said that son of a bitch is a *fiddle* player?" Umstead smiled.

CRENSHAW SAT AT his desk in his office. It was almost time to go in. He looked out the window at the uneven paint job on the side of his garage, at the grove of pines beyond that. The shadow of the church moved halfway up the pines and the sun shone dull orange on their top halves.

In the end, he'd not written to Cheryl Daniels. He had found victory, had repented, and had prepared a major sermon for tonight. He hadn't been able to wait until next Sunday. Mrs. Clark had been a part of his getting turned around. *She* had written *him* a note saying she had accidentally seen his letter to a young lady of the church, and had turned it all over to Jesus. She wouldn't tell anybody. Jesus, thought Crenshaw, had seen to it that Mrs. Clark see that letter, and had seen to the right obstacles being put in the right places on his journey down the first mile or two of a very low road. Mrs. Clark would hear his sermon—and would understand. She was slow, but not dumb. She would understand that he had been sorely tempted by the Devil, had almost fallen, and was now back on track with the Lord. It all could have, if not terminated, led to an outrage—the breakup of his marriage, even. The loss of his church! He had been brought by the living spirit of Jesus Christ through prayer to *know* that. Mrs. Clark would get the message of his turnabout—loud and clear—and then afterward there would be no mention of that letter, no need for explanations. Would there? What if she didn't believe him? He'd never took the time to get to know Mrs. Clark very well. She was odd somehow, with her marriage to Claude T., and her medicines, and this way she had of living in her office. He never quite knew what she might do next. Plus he kept forgetting she was over there. And he'd already gotten a call from Donna Walker asking if the church should be getting *rent* from Mrs. Clark.

Cheryl would be out there in the congregation in a few minutes. And if she had been thinking what he thought she had been thinking, through the influence of the Devil, then tonight—through his sermon—she would get the message; yes, by golly, it was necessary that she get the NO message loud and clear. Prayer—and circumstances planted by God—had saved him, were in the process of saving him as he sat staring through the window at good wholesome church people, the Livingston family, walking from the parking lot behind his garage to prayer meeting. His call was from God and unto *them,* not to himself and the sinful impulses fed to him by the Devil.

STEPHEN TOOMEY ALREADY knew in his young life that if he heard the call, a call that all people received at some time in their lives, then he should walk down front and tell Preacher Crenshaw that he believed in God and Jesus. That was how you got saved—but only if Jesus called. Jesus called everybody at one time or another and those who didn't answer, those who didn't go down front and accept Jesus, were going to hell when they died. His mama had told him that. Mr. Sellers, his Sunday school teacher, had told him that, and Mr. Crenshaw had told Stephen's whole Sunday school class that, twice. Getting saved was a little bit like another kind of once-in-a-lifetime chance that would come when he grew up: there was that one woman in the world made for each man. You would find her and marry her and have children. His mama had told him that and read to him about it in *Aunt Margaret's Bible Stories,* and she'd told him some other things, too. But first you had to answer Jesus—that came first—and you'd better be ready when He called. He was out there somewhere, just beyond the walls of the church, deciding who to call. And when He came through the church wall and called you, all you had to do was believe and go down front and say so. Believe in God and the Lord Jesus Christ and you go to heaven when you die.

Stephen had spent pieces of many days driving his cars and trucks in the dirt out back at their garage. He'd built roads and hills. The trucks turned around, backed up. They turned over. They had bad wrecks. It all might as well have been true—the roads and hills—and then . . . then he'd learned the very first for-real-sure-true thing in the world. Heaven. And to get there you had to be good, but that wouldn't do it. You had to believe in Jesus. And this he did. To not believe meant eternal death for sure. All he had to do now was wait to be called down to the front. If he missed the call, God would call him once again maybe, but if he refused to answer, then . . . in his almost seven years on earth he'd looked into burning grass, piles of burning wood. He'd even looked into the big fire of burning tires and felt the awful heat. He knew about hell.

CRENSHAW WALKED IN, onto the podium, and sat down in his chair. He scanned the congregation. His own family was in the right place, second row left. Paul was too fidgety. Marjorie would get after him.

He looked for Cheryl. She didn't always sit in the same place. He saw Mrs. Clark behind Alease Toomey. There was Cheryl coming in the back, almost late. His eyes had minds of their own. He pulled them back to his wife. Temptation comes to every man, over and over, and every woman—it came to Eve, but she failed—and it came to Jesus and Jesus stood strong. Think of what-all Jesus could have had as a man. He could have had the world and everything in it. He could have had a thousand Cheryl Danielses, for a thousand nights each. But He had not allowed that to interest Him the least bit.

There was a new face—a man in wire-rimmed glasses.

Talmadge Scully, down front, brought the congregation to its feet to sing the opening hymn.

As he sang, Doug Harmon remembered that he'd forgot to buy his daddy a pack of Dr. Scholl's small corn pads that afternoon. / Fred Quin visualized the long bent nail he'd pulled out of his tractor tire with his pliers. He worried about Bob Sanders not seeming to want to come over and help him load the tire into his pickup to take up to Puttman's Tire. / Irene Rogers shifted her weight so that her left knee hurt less. She wondered why that new woman had looked at her funny when Irene told everybody in Sunday school she'd been in every state except Delaware. She looked like she resented it. / Little Zalph Loggins finally found a piece of gum under the pew that he *could* get his fingernail under. He popped it off, looked at it, and decided not to chew it. Then he wondered what kind it might be and decided to go ahead. He put it in his mouth to see if it was Juicy Fruit. It was Dentyne he believed, so he took it back out and tried to stick it back under the pew. It wouldn't hold. He put it in a hymnbook. He looked up at one of the hanging lights and held his eyes to it so everything in the big room would finally whiten out. / Little Tina Pascall swallowed her Life Saver and wondered if it could get around her heart and

stop it from beating. Her mama was always saying, "Bless your little heart. Bless your little
heart." She tugged at her mama's skirt. Her mama
gave her a hard look. She tugged again. Her
mother bent down to listen.

Crenshaw's text was Matthew 4:1–11. He led in prayer,
read the Scripture, then preached:

"Jesus had been in the desert for forty days and nights; He
was tired. Tired and hungry. *Famished,* in fact." Crenshaw's
body tensed and he clenched his fist on the word "famished."

"The Devil tempted Him to turn *stones* into bread. Jesus
re*fus*ed. The Devil tempted Jesus to *throw* Himself off the
temple, and show *every*body that God was protecting Him.
Jesus re*fus*ed."

Long pause. He walked from behind the lectern, to the
edge of the podium, paused, looked out at all the faces looking back. They were listening well. The Spirit was speaking
through him. "The Devil showed Jesus *all* the kingdoms of
the world"—arm sweep—"and said that if Jesus would simply *worship him, worship the Devil,* then he would *give* those
kingdoms to Jesus. Jesus re*fus*ed, the Devil *left* Him, and
angels—angels administered unto Jesus." Crenshaw returned
to the pulpit, looked at Cheryl, gathered himself together,

said a short, hard, silent prayer to God. Cleared his mind of her.

STEPHEN REMEMBERED THE picture of Jesus standing on the hill looking at all the cities the Devil owned. The Devil was standing behind Jesus. The Devil, mean and evil and nasty and blue, was offering gentle white Jesus the whole world, just to do something wrong. And Jesus held strong even though He was weak and tired and hungry from forty days in the desert without anything to drink or eat. Not the first little cracker crumb. Stephen loved Jesus for being so strong, for saying no. Jesus was perfect—He could have been a prison guard one time.

CRENSHAW FELT THE power of his redemption, his rededication, his partnership with Jesus. He looked briefly at Mrs. Clark. Would God touch her, tell her it was okay to never for sure mention that letter? He would have a brief word with her after the service and explain—if she didn't get it—his redemption in ways connected to that letter. Clearly connected. She would understand.

He preached of temptations that all men, all women, all children face every single day of their lives. Christian, sinner, Gentile, Jew. The temptation to do wrong. Some people fight it, some don't. And God's messengers—preachers—face it too. They get it just like everybody else, sometimes worse. They get temptation dressed in all kinds of tempting colors and, and flavors. "The *Devil* is not unschooled, the *Devil* is not ignorant, the *Devil* is *smart,* smart as a *whip*. The *Devil* was once *Ga*-hood's right-hand *angel*. The *Devil* knows the human *mind* and the human *heart* and can pa-*lay* it like a fiddle."

FIDDLE, JACK UMSTEAD thought. I won't sitting beside . . . and I won't sitting beside . . .

"I . . . I . . . EVEN I have wrestled with the Devil—to*day*. I came to a *draw*. To a *draw,* dear friend, because dear friend you do not *beat* the Devil. The Devil bounces *back* . . . and *back* . . . and *back again* . . . But finally, dear friends, with the help of Jesus Christ, I won. I won the battle, but only for a while. The Devil will be back. Yet again." Pause. "Yet again," he said softly. Then he whispered: "Yet again. The tragedy will be played again, and again. And without Jesus, without"—he shouted, now—"*Jesus* in your *heart* you will *lose* the battle, and the *price* of that loss will be an e*ternity* in *hell,* where *thirst* is everlasting, where *hunger* is everlasting, where *poverty* is everlasting, where *pain* is everlasting, where *darkness* . . . and horror . . . and sadness are everlasting. Everlasting . . . even unto everlasting."

Crenshaw—pacing, pointing to heaven, to hell—spelled out, spilled out the awful love of Jesus, the awful need to come to Jesus, the awful need to place your hand in the nail-scarred hand.

MRS. CLARK FELT Preacher Crenshaw's torment. He had been through an event that brought Jesus to Listre, and Jesus had saved his life. That had to be it. Preacher Crenshaw had clearly had a visit from Jesus, too. No man could preach like that if he hadn't been visited by Jesus. Preacher Crenshaw was on fire for God. Yes, Jesus was in Listre. And she had talked to Him. Even if He was there to talk to Preacher Crenshaw, she had been just as privileged as he had. Jesus had come all the way from the Middle Ages straight to her and her pastor. What a wonderful world it had turned out to be. Claude T. might even back off his Cadillac and diamond ring a little bit what with Jesus nearby and all.

CRENSHAW, DURING THE invitation hymn, asked the choir to hum the second stanza of "Just as I Am." Holding his hand in the air, he told the congregation how much Jesus loved them each and every one. He could feel Jesus stirring among them. The congregation was mostly silent—only the slightest rustling of handheld fans. Two people had come down to give their lives to Jesus and there had been three rededications. "Jesus is here among us. Will you come? Will you come?"

And then the third stanza started . . . so slowly, oh, so slowly: *Just as I am* . . .

STEPHEN FELT JESUS' fingers gently touch his heart. The music was touching his cheeks, his whole face. The whole big room was full of Jesus and music. The color of Jesus was a smokey gray. Jesus was there in his head and in his heart, floating around, calling out—Come, come, come. It was happening. He could almost, but not quite, see Jesus. Jesus was whispering into his heart, words that were not words, words that acted, tugged at him, drawing him down toward the front, down to give his heart to Jesus, down toward Preacher Crenshaw, God's man on earth. Mrs. Clark with her four-footed cane started a slow hobble down to the preacher, who extended his arms to her, hugged her. She whispered into his ear. He whispered back. She whispered again. He whispered back and smiled at her and hugged her again.

Stephen watched. Mr. Crenshaw said to the congregation, "Take that first step, take that first step, take that *first* step." The *gypsy man* brushed by, walking down the aisle, his head down. Stephen stepped into the aisle and Jesus was in him, leading him every step of the way. He was in Jesus. He felt like he was going to cry because he loved Jesus so much. Jesus was saving him.

JACK UMSTEAD HAD joined churches before. He'd even got on a committee one time.

STEPHEN, STANDING BEHIND the gypsy man, was crying. Jesus was all around him. Mrs. Clark was hobbling past him back to her seat. She put her hand on his shoulder, bent her head to his, put her mouth to his ear. "God bless you, son. God bless you." He looked into her eyes, through the thumb-printed glasses that made her eyes look as big as her head.

CRENSHAW PUT HIS arm over the shoulder of the new man. God was surely moving in this crowd. A stranger—come to Jesus.

"Preacher, I'm a lost soul. I want to give my heart and soul to Jesus. I'm a sinner and I want to be saved of my own free will."

"Do you believe, friend, that God so loved the world that He gave His only begotten son, that—"

"Whosoever believeth in Him should not perish but have everlasting life. I do, Preacher. I do."

"God bless you. Just have a seat. Fill out the form on the clipboard there. God bless you." A little boy was next. The Toomey boy. God was moving in this crowd. Praise God.

"Yes, son. Steve, is it?"

"Yessir. I love Jesus so much that I know he loves me too."

"Do you accept Jesus as your personal saviour—believe that God so loved the world that he gave His only begotten son that whosoever believeth in Him should not perish but have everlasting life?"

"Yessir, I do." The boy was crying.

"God bless you, son."

ALEASE MOVED DOWN onto the front row to be with Stephen. Her main prayer in the world had been answered. Her son had been saved. She had dedicated Stephen's life to Jesus Christ just after he was born and now God's will was being shown. The final act had happened. Her son was saved. Now all that awaited was his living his life as Jesus led him.

Now what could it mean that Mr. Jones was down there, too? When he came for yard work, would they talk about this?

"Stephen, honey, don't cry. Jesus loves you. I'm so proud of you. Jesus loves you."

WHERE TROUBLE SLEEPS

FRIDAY NOON AT Train's Place, Jack Umstead asked Blake where Trouble took his morning nap. Inside.

Just after the first distant thunder on Friday afternoon, Umstead pulled into the driveway at the Toomey house. The sun was still shining, but that dark cloud was sitting heavy in the west and moving in low and slow. The time had come. He almost wasn't glad. And he wanted to finish his work in the flower garden by the garage, get another glass of iced tea.

Then he'd stop by Train's Place for a Blatz just for the hell of it, and then on over to the grill to see Cheryl. By then it would be raining and he could make his move. He might as well tell Cheryl that they'd get married soon. That would give her something to look forward to for the rest of her life, and if he didn't have all his mental and nerve problems, by God he would marry her. She didn't have no connections, she liked dirty movies, she was beautiful to look at, she'd had sense enough to graduate from high school, she loved to choke his chicken, and it seemed like she really meant what she said.

Seven-year-old Sally Creightenberry was starting her piano competition down at Mrs. Williams's house. Listening was a judge from Memphis, Tennessee, and some other students. Her song was "In Frog Land." The first six notes were two C major chord triads, starting on the C below middle C. The next three notes were the first triad repeated. Then the tenth note was to be a low G, a fourth below her first note. However, for some reason she hit a low C, an octave below her first note. It seemed the correct thing to do, but was clearly and horribly wrong. She'd never done that in her life—that is, made something sound as if the whole piano had changed on her. Something had gone wrong, something *had* changed, but she couldn't understand what. Surely she'd hit the right note. But it sounded completely out of whack. She sat for a few seconds, started again. The same thing happened again! Her neck was suddenly very hot and the little musical village in her mind crumbled, pieces completely out of place, strange pieces in view. She brought her hands to her face and cried as silently as she could, knowing Mrs. Williams would be right there in a few seconds to get her out of this awful mess where other students and a judge all the way from Memphis, Tennessee, had listened and heard, and seen. / Mr. Weams had eaten everything on his dinner plate and Mrs. Weams was trying to get him to eat more of everything. He was saying no, no, no. She said, "Don't you want some more pintos? I didn't give you but about six." "Well, yes," he said, "I'll take another six."

After stopping at the Toomey house, Train's Place, and the grill, tending to business at all three places, and with the rain pounding—Trouble was right again—Umstead drove by the Blaine sisters' garage to be sure their car was gone. It was, and the crossroads seemed fairly deserted except the damn Toomey kid was sitting on the grocery store bench and several beer drinkers stood under the shelter at Train's, so he parked out of sight beyond the Blaine sisters' store, walked around behind it, and trudged up through the gully back there, kicked in the downstairs door, splintering it at the lock, and entered their living quarters.

Cats were all over the place, some rubbing up against his leg and some backing off, watching him. Mr. Three-Legs. "Well, look at you, Mr. Three-Legs." The rain blew in, a light spray. He pulled the lightbulb string in the middle of the room, walked back over and closed the door. He'd tracked in yellow mud.

Little .410 shotgun leaning in the corner. He wondered if it was loaded, picked it up, unbreeched it. Damn. Loaded. He breeched it and put it back, then decided to steal the shell for the hell of it, for a surprise next time they went to shoot a chicken.

The room looked about like he expected: couch, couple of big soft chairs, very lived-in, chest of drawers, a place to cook, icebox, narrow flight of stairs up to the store part. In the bedroom, the bed all made up, two valleys in the mattress like there might be two invisible old women lying there asleep.

Back in the sitting room, he got right to work: pulled open the top drawer to the chest of drawers, kicked a cat. The place smelled like cats.

The lightning flashed a double flash. Silence. Thunder

boomed, tumbled and rumbled and tumbled. The rain beat hard on the tin roof, against the windowpane, let up, beat harder, then let up again.

STEPHEN WATCHED THE men across the way. One turned up his bottle and drank several long swallows of beer. He was probably letting it gurgle. It was raining too hard to tell for sure. Stephen turned up his Big Top, but he kept his mouth tight on the opening. He was afraid to relax and drink that other way. He might spill it all over.

The men stood around and talked to each other, laughed like they were talking nasty, bent over at the waist, stepped back, stood up straight, and turned up their beer bottles. Stephen could see them silent behind moving sheets of rain.

He stood up, held his Big Top down by his side loosely like they did, as if about to drop it. He said, "A cow has great big titties." Something kind of dirty. Something one of them might say.

INSIDE THE GROCERY store, Harvey reached into the drink box and pulled out a Coke from standing cold water, opened it in the opener, got a BC powder from the wall behind the cash register, held the V-shaped paper to his mouth, turned it up, took a long swig of Coke, opened the cash register, dropped in a quarter and took out a dime. There was a business predictability about this store he liked for his brother to be in charge of. You buy goods, you sell goods, you make some money. You do a good job and you get more and more customers. It was the kind of work that would help Steve settle down some, now that the war was over and he was back home. It was what he needed. Harvey himself wouldn't have minded running the grocery full-time, but it was going to work out best with him just helping out until Steve got himself settled down, maybe married. Harvey's own regular job at Liggett & Myers was right for him. Nine to five. This grocery store with a little luck could offer security for Steve. Harvey knew his mama and papa would be much more satisfied in life if Steve settled down.

BEA HAD BEEN sitting for a while with Mae and Dorothea in the church office, when she realized she'd forgotten her pocketbook. The church janitor, Andrew, drove her right up under the shelter that was over the front door of the store and let her out. She opened the store's front door at about the same time something slammed down below. A dresser drawer it sounded like. She caught her breath. Somebody rummaging around down there? It ran all over her. *Somebody had picked this time, knowing they'd be gone.* Some coward thief, somebody that had made fun of her and Mae for leaving during thunderstorms, she bet. Some coward.

UMSTEAD KEPT GOING at it, now in the pantry looking through everything with a lid or in a bag, just making a great big mess, flour and cornmeal and rice all in the floor. He remembered his grandma's pantry, the big glass jars of flour and cornmeal and rice, the keg of molasses and how she had tied him up by his thumbs for stealing molasses, and how she would rock him to sleep sometimes.

BEA BLAINE HAD long ago driven two big nails in the staircase wall—to hold the big shotgun, the 12-gauge, always loaded. She had figured that's the only place it would do them any good in case they were in one part of the building, up or down, and a robber in the other. So on the way downstairs, leaving Andrew out in her car with the motor running, Bea calmly pulled the shotgun down off the wall—the same shotgun she used on mercy cats on an occasional New Year's Eve. Mae always said use the .410, but Bea liked sure results.

She stood on the second step from the bottom and aimed down those thirty-four-inch double barrels into the pantry at the center of a yellow shirt back. "Come out of there," she said.

JACK UMSTEAD LOOKED over his shoulder with calmness, an assurance that all would be well. He was, however, not expecting to be looking up the double barrels of a 12-gauge shotgun. He'd already thought in a flash—when he heard her voice—that he'd just walk out, and if she got in the way, simply push her down, walk to his car, and drive on out of there. He never ran. You should always look like you were supposed to be doing exactly what you were doing. But he hadn't counted on a gun, here. Like this.

He said, "You better put that down."

"No sir. You pick up that broom and that dustpan in there and you get up ever bit of that flour and stuff outen that pantry floor. Dump it in that trash can in there. You lowlife pond scum."

Aw hell, she was plenty mad and he didn't want to sweep no floor. He hadn't swept a floor in so long he couldn't remember. He reached for the broom, thought about flinging it at her—while ducking and rolling for the door. He started sweeping, his back to her. He figured maybe he'd sweep up a full dustpan of flour, get a little closer to her, and throw it in her face. That's what he'd do.

"You remind me of my grandma," he said, holding the dustpan full of flour and rice, looking at her.

• • •

"IS THAT RIGHT? Well, you ain't no kin to me. And some-body didn't whip you enough. If you got spanked every day of your life then you wouldn't a turned out like you have. I thought from the beginning something was wrong with you."

"Miss Bea?" said a voice from the stairs.

She heard Andrew coming down the steps one at a time, very slowly, dropping one foot, then the other.

"I was wondering," said Andrew, "where you—oh, my goodness gracious."

"Sit down, Andrew. Sit down right there on the steps. I caught this chicken-thief red-handed." She lowered the shot-gun to waist level. Her arms were getting tired and shaking a little bit.

The no-count looked at her.

"Don't get no ideas," she said. She made a little push motion with the gun. "I'll shoot a hole in you big enough to stick my arm through."

HE COULD WALK toward her and simply take the gun. He could, on the other hand, just walk out and leave her standing there. Or he could kill them both. There was an ice pick stuck in the wall by the stairs. He could stab her, shoot him, pull off his pants, or some combination, and it would look like they killed each other.

"What are we going to do when I finish cleaning up this floor?" he asked. He wanted bad now to get on the road before any authorities got involved. He did *not* want to deal with any authorities.

"I'm going to let you clean up the rest of this mess you've made. You ought to be ashamed of yourself. Look at that bedroom."

Now she was off the stairs, down on the level floor, a couple of steps closer.

"You want me to call the sheriff, Miss Bea?" asked the Andrew man.

"No, Andrew, we don't need the sheriff. I got a better idea. We're going to take him out back after he finishes cleaning up his mess and let him dig his grave."

He tried to kind of laugh it off, but his voice refused him. Something had taken over this skinny old woman. She was moving now like she wadn't so old, after all.

"But, ah, Miss Mae said for us to come straight back and not to stop nowhere."

"Listen, that thing could go off," said Umstead. "If you're going to shoot me, I ain't going to clean up in here. Let's just get it over with." He raised his hands and smiled a little bit for the first time.

"Let me tell you what we do on New Year's Eve sometimes," she said, narrowing her slitty eyes. "We take the one or two mercy cats, ones that's lived out their time, and we take them out there in that gully where you tracked in all that mud from, and we shoot them in the head and then bury them. That's what I'm fixing to do with you, except I ain't got no hole dug. Yet. And I'll tell you this: It's not no pretty sight."

"Well," said Jack Umstead. He looked to Andrew. Andrew's face was blank. He turned back to the pantry, placed the dustpan full of flour and rice on the middle shelf just inside the pantry door. He could throw it in her face when he made a run for it, or when she got closer to him. She was a tad too far away to make a move, yet. He'd wait. One time he worked for a man in Greenville, Mississippi, who had a big sign on his office wall that said WAIT.

"Miss Bea," said Andrew, "I don't think you ought to shoot him. We need to call Sheriff Frazier."

"You," she said to Umstead. "You reach back in that pantry and you empty that dustpan in that trash can in there."

He was going to have to figure out something else. She was smart. He emptied the dustpan. He would probably end up just walking out. But he needed some insurance—he needed to make her feel sorry for him. "You need to know I've been saved, Miss Blaine. Wednesday night. I repented. I've had a real hard life. I could show you some scars, and then

just this Wednesday night I accepted Jesus Christ as my personal saviour right down here at the church, and this here
today is a consequence of some backsliding. Everybody back-
slides. Don't you go to church down there?"

"I don't go to church. I'm a Methodist."

"Well see, the boys over at Train's dared me to come in
here and steal a little something. Just a prank. Just a old boy's
prank. And the truth is, I'm a true Christian now. That's the
truth. So help me God. And I'll tell you something else. I
could use a drink of water."

"We're going outside now."

> Mrs. Taggart was trying to remember the last
> time she had a bath. Could she wait another day
> or two? / Mrs. Louise Perry was standing in
> front of her new refrigerator. It was making funny
> noises. That was the second time in two days.
> Somebody said Wilma Morgan had unplugged
> one to keep it quiet.

In the gully, in the rain, Jack Umstead placed the point of
the shovel against the yellow mud. The point disappeared.
Two little rivers of rainwater ran down the side of his face. He
placed his foot on the shovel and pushed it on down into the

mud. It sank to its shaft. He shoveled mud—a loud sucking sound. The hole filled back in by half, mud running in like lava. He shoveled again. My God, there was a . . . wet matted fur, ass-end of a cat. This had gone far enough.

The old bitch was standing on a little mound covered with pinestraw about, what, fifteen feet away, getting wet herself, though the rain had eased up considerably, now just a drizzle. Something had come over her and it didn't look good. Some green leaves blew across the ground—a gust of wind that made him remember duck hunting, which made him remember the name for a group of crows: a murder of crows. The storm had shook loose some green leaves. This would turn out okay. It was just a little more complicated than he'd counted on. That Andrew. Why the hell didn't he go get somebody? Three cats were coming down there, moving slowly like they knew something was going to happen.

"You're going to catch your death of cold out here," he told her.

She was holding the shotgun level at her waist. "You dig." She lifted the shotgun to her shoulder, aimed right at his face. "Andrew, how about this?" she said.

The rain eased up some more, then stopped. The thunder was far away. The wind was still.

He'd just have to go ahead and call her bluff.

"I don't think I can dig anymore," he said. He stood in the mud looking at her one open eye beyond the BB and the little V between the double zeroes of the gun barrels. She was steady and god-awful. She might as well be a man.

"You're going to have to shoot me now," he said. He estimated the distance between them. "I'm not going to die the fool. I'll be glad for you to shoot me, but I ain't dying the fool. So you just go ahead and shoot me now. Dear God, oh dear God above," he said, looking up. He raised one hand, leaned on the shovel. "Forgive me all my sins. Bless me and keep me and all the poor forgotten souls on this earth." At that instant the sun came out. "See," he said. "See that. God heard me. You saw that. It was just like a miracle. For God so loved the world—"

"You *look* like a man," she said. "You *look* like a man."

"—believeth in him should not perish but have . . ."

AT THE GROCERY store, Stephen asked his daddy if he could go ahead over to the Blaines'. Miss Bea had told him he could shoot a chicken that afternoon, and the rain was over, and she'd already come home. His daddy told him to remember to keep it on safety until he pulled the trigger.

Stephen found the door open to the upstairs store part, but nobody in there, so he walked back outside, down, and around to the back, where he came upon a scene: the gypsy man, soaking wet, with yellow mud on his trouser legs, digging a big hole, and Miss Bea aiming a big, different kind of shotgun at him. A double-barrel. She looked kind of wet, too. Why were they wet?

"Well, hey, son," said Miss Bea. "You stand right there. This Mr. Jones here turns out to be a common thief. He's already robbed us inside, now he's out here digging for more."

"Listen, Budrow," said the gypsy man. His voice sounded dry and kind of high. "Bring me that four-ten from inside right now. I'm going to shoot a chicken for Miss Blaine here. She's just playing a—"

"Andrew," said Miss Bea, "get that four-ten. Little Steve, son, you stay where you are."

"Ah, Miss Bea," said Andrew, "I don't think—"

Umstead saw that for the first time the 12-gauge was not pointing at him, and as he made his charge, he thought of that lovely lonely Toomey woman. Good enough to eat. She loved him, he bet. She had—

KA-BLOOM!

• • •

THE SUN BROKE through even brighter, bright enough to hurt Stephen's eyes. The gypsy man had slipped in the mud and reached for the ground just before the explosion went right into the top of his head. He was on the ground, blood, his arm twitching. And then: KA-BLOOM! *again*. She'd been aiming right down the barrels. As he lay on the ground, still, the blood and hair let go little whiffs of smoke.

THE FIRST BLAST scared the hell out of the cats. Always did. They couldn't get it straight in their knowledge when a bad noise was coming. There was no warning smell or sound or single thing to warn them so they could scat. It plain bothered them. They ran for cover, then BOOM—again!

"What the hell?" "That sounded like a twelve-gauge." "Sure did. And they already back after the storm?" "What the hell they doing shooting chickens with a twelve-gauge?"

MISS BEA WAS sitting on the ground. The gypsy man was lying on the ground with blood and something white flowing out, and those little whiffs of smoke. The cats had gone running off. Miss Bea was sitting down looking off in the trees and Andrew was leaving. Stephen felt the asthma coming. He turned and ran, his chest tightening. Bottle caps under his feet in the grocery store parking lot. Inside, he told his daddy and Uncle Steve and they both walked very fast over toward the Blaine sisters' store. He looked both ways, ran across the road. Nobody was outside over there. He walked into the dark inside. He felt something wonderful and scary. Mr. Blake and Mr. Luke were sitting in chairs, and over behind the candy counter was Mr. Train in his wheelchair.

"What's the matter, son?"

"Miss Bea, she just shot the gypsy man."

"What!?"

Mr. Blake stood.

Stephen would have to go tell Cheryl because she and the gypsy man were going to get married so she could wear a white dress. They had that secret together. He looked on the wall and there was the naked woman wearing a cowboy hat and cowboy boots. She had great big smooth naked titties and a big smile on her face. He kept looking. He needed to go tell Cheryl. Then he had to tell his mama. He was going to have to cross the road again.

"Where's he at?" asked Mr. Train.

"Down at the chicken pen."

"Is he just wounded or did she shoot him good?"

"She shot him good. In the head." Stephen had seen it in

the movies, but never with the blood and the other like that. He looked at the woman on the wall again. He took his eyes away. He had accepted Jesus as his saviour. It was wrong to look. He had to hurry to Cheryl. They had that secret.

Mr. Luke and Mr. Blake walked out past him.

"Was she shooting a chicken?" asked Mr. Train.

"She was shooting him."

"On purpose?"

"Yessir."

"Why?"

"I don't know. He run at her with a shovel."

"Damn."

Mr. Train wheeled over to the telephone.

Stephen headed for the grill—for Cheryl. When he walked through the door he saw her behind the counter setting a cup of coffee on the counter for a man in a ball cap.

Cheryl looked at him. "What's wrong, Stephen?"

"Miss Bea just shot the gypsy man."

Cheryl came out from behind the counter, walked over to Stephen, knelt down in front of him. "What? She did what?"

"She shot the gypsy man in the top of the head."

"The gypsy man? Oh Lord. Stephen. Are you sure? Is he hurt bad?"

"He looked like he was dead."

"Oh, my God. Where is he?"

"Down at the chicken pen."

"Oh, my God." Cheryl went running out. Stephen turned to watch her go.

"What did you say?" the man in the ball cap said. "Somebody got shot?"

"The gypsy man."

THE GYPSY MAN'S TEA

CHERYL RAN AROUND the back corner of the
Blaine sisters' store. Two small groups of men. One around a
man on the ground, wet, facedown. Delbert? "Delbert?"
Somebody stepped, brown trousers, so she couldn't see the
head, the face. In the other group, somebody was helping
Miss Bea up to her feet, taking a shotgun from her. Cheryl
looked back. Then she did see. It was Delbert, perfectly still,
not moving, very quiet. Eyes *open*. Blood, blood. Nobody was
touching him. She was pulled to him, to kneel, but repelled
by the death around him as if it, the death, were a visible,
stinking cloud. She started to kneel, then stood, immobile,
collapsing inside like the inward rock walls of a deep well
falling down into the water, filling it, and then filling the
opening until there was no room even for air in what was the

long tall cool opening that you could once look down into and see the water reflecting the sky.

ALEASE DIDN'T BELIEVE Stephen until she got on the phone and called Harvey at the store and he told her it was true, that there had been a robbery at the Blaine sisters', and the Settle Inn man, Jones, was shot dead. Big Steve was over there.

She hung up the phone.

"You *saw* it, son?"

"Yes ma'am." Stephen was sitting on the couch holding his bottle at his side. His mother stood.

"How do you know he was Cheryl's boyfriend?"

"She told me."

"Are you sure that's who it was?"

"Yes ma'am. It was the gypsy man."

Alease looked around the room, then sat down. "Did you know he was robbing the Blaine sisters—trying to steal their money?"

"No ma'am. He was just digging a hole."

"He was just digging a hole?—no, that's not what happened, son. Something had already happened when you got there. Daddy said he was a robber and we didn't know that . . . You *saw* her shoot him?"

"Yes ma'am."

"Oh, Stephen. Oh, my goodness. You lie down and rest, and I'll make some phone calls. There goes the ambulance."

Somebody might have to go to the electric chair about all this, Stephen thought. Miss Bea probably wouldn't, though. She was just a old lady. He wondered about Uncle Raleigh, for being the way he was, if he kept on being that way. "Miss Bea broke the Ten Commandments."

"What?"

"Miss Bea broke the Ten Commandments."

"No, not exactly, not when somebody is robbing your house. Now you just try to rest. I'm going to call June."

"Why didn't the Blaine sisters ever get married? Then a man would have been there."

"I don't know, son. You just try to rest, now. Don't be asking questions."

"I thought they always left during the rain. It was raining, won't it?" "She come back home for her pocketbook for some reason and caught him digging in the backyard. Looking for something. He must of knew something nobody else did." "He'd already been through the house and store, tore it all up in there." "Was it a nigger?" "No, it was somebody staying at the Settle Inn. A Jones, from T.R. He'd done joined Listre Baptist for some reason and was staying at the Settle Inn." "I seen him in the grill. He'd been coming in there for breakfast. He'd been in there the last three mornings. He had one of them pencil-thin mustaches." "He had the hots for Cheryl Daniels." "He was a peculiar man. He sat right here on this bench and asked me all about my ring and about my car. I should of known he was up to something." "He asked me about putting in the blinker light, and then when I told him he changed the subject."

Alease called June to come over and sit with Stephen for fifteen minutes. When June got there, Alease told her what had happened, got Stephen settled, then walked down to the grocery. People were milling around everywhere—coming and going to the chicken pen in a line like ants. A black hearse was backed up down there. Sitting by herself on the bench at the grocery store was Cheryl. Alease sat down beside her. Cheryl's eyes were bloodshot. She wouldn't look at Alease.

"What happened, Cheryl?"

"Miss Bea shot Delbert Jones. He's dead. He's dead."

"Why did she do that? . . . Do you know why?"

247

"They said he was robbing her." Cheryl drew into herself as if she were cold. "I don't know what I'm going to do now. We had these plans, but I can't tell anybody, Mrs. Toomey." Then she looked from one of Alease's eyes to the other, back and forth.

"Let me get your hat, honey," said Alease. "It's out of place." She unpinned it. "Here."

Cheryl looked over at Train's. Alease followed her eyes. There was nobody over there. "But I can't tell anybody," said Cheryl. "Especially not now. I don't think he would have robbed anybody, and even if he did, how could . . . I want . . . could you . . . would you take me up to the funeral home?" she pleaded. "Wayside got him. Could you maybe take me up there? I know he did some work for you."

"I don't know. I hadn't . . . I suppose I could."

"I don't want my daddy to find out." Her hands were clasped together, one wringing the other.

"I'll . . . I'll help you out. I'm real sorry, Cheryl."

"He meant everything to me, Mrs. Toomey."

ANDREW, EATING SUPPER at home, told his wife, Flo, how he'd pulled in a couch from the preacher's office and another from the library so all three women could stay in the church that night. Mrs. Weams had brought enough sheets and blankets for everybody. Mrs. Clark's husband had brought them a pint of strawberry ice cream each.

Then Andrew and Flo talked more about the shooting.

"Why didn't you just go call the sheriff anyway?" asked Flo.

"I wadn't sure who had a telephone."

"Well, it look like to me you could have just gone anywhere and ask somebody where was there a telephone."

"I was *with* Miss Bea, Flo. You know good and well I just couldn't leave her with no *robber*."

"Sound like you shouldn't have left no robber with *her*."

"Well, I didn't care if she shot him or not."

"Andrew!"

"He was a robber. But I kept asking her could I go call the sheriff."

"What you going to say now if the sheriff ask you what happen?"

"He done ask me and I told him what Miss Blaine said—that he trashed up the whole inside of the house and was digging up the yard when she walked out there with the shotgun and he come at her. That actually in fact was the way it was. And that little boy showed up and saw the whole thing. She got him right in top of the head. His feet slipped in the mud and just about the time his hand hit the ground—he kind of reached down to catch hisself, see——and that's when he caught the whole load in the top of his head. He dropped and bounced a little bounce and his arm jerked around some and she shot him again. Whew. Like shooting a snake. Lord have mercy. I ain't never seen nothing like it."

STEPHEN'S MOTHER, HOLDING his hand, said pretty much the same prayer as always that night. "Dear God, help us to love one another. Help us to accept each other for better or worse, in sickness and in death. Help us to understand Thy will in our lives, and we pray that Stephen may grow up with a purpose in life that is worthy of a Christian gentleman. And we pray for the soul of Mr. Jones, and we accept Thy reasons for all that happens on this earth. In Jesus' name. Amen. Stephen?"

"Dear God, thank you for Inky and may he be safe in heaven. Thank you for keeping us safe from the gypsy man. Now I lay me down to sleep I pray the Lord my soul to keep if I should die before I wake I pray the Lord my soul to take if I should live another day I pray the Lord to show the way. Amen."

"'Night, Harvey."

"'Night. Was he by here this afternoon?"

"Who?"

"Jones."

"Yes. He stopped by. He was looking for work, he said."

"Well . . . I'm glad Miss Bea's got her sisters. You just can't ever tell."

NEXT DAY, CRENSHAW listened. There she was. Cheryl. Sitting in a chair in his office.

"Preacher Crenshaw, I don't have anybody I can go to to talk about this. And I didn't know anything about him being a robber or anything. He had a good heart, Preacher Crenshaw. There had to be some kind of mix-up."

Her eyes were red-rimmed. She had a Kleenex in her hand. She was twisting it apart.

Crenshaw leaned forward, elbows on his desk. He was embarrassed that he had to see her almost out of control like this, and aware of what it looked like the man had done to her, or with her.

The Devil's voice: "Crenshaw, stand up. Go around that desk. You can have it *too*. It's all yours. She wants it. She wants it too. She wants you. Give that young thing a hug. Hug her all up tight and whisper in her ear that everything is going to be all right and then see if you feel her moving at all and if she's moving in the right way you'll know it. And if she's not, you can wait till next time—or get her to move in the right way."

"Cheryl, I am sorry that this . . . happened. I just had a call about it all and they found out that his car was stolen. We never know. He certainly may have been a Christian. We can't say." He started to get up, but didn't. "I never dreamed he'd do something like that. And it looks like he took advantage of you." And God was telling him to tell her to rededicate her life to Jesus. He thought about the woman at the well. "What you did, Cheryl, you did out of love," he said. "That's all. What you did was normal, and what is normal can't ever be sin enough to send you to hell. That's my own thought on that. I've been wrestling with all this. I'm sorry this has all happened and anytime I can listen, you can come on in here and just talk. I've always had a particular liking for you. But you should know you can feel safe with me. I like your heart. I'm partial to your heart."

"Thank you, Mr. Crenshaw."

She stood and turned, headed for the door. He sat still, looked at a picture of roses on the wall beside the door, and then closed his eyes. So many people depended on him. He had to be strong.

Edward Cates was trying to fall asleep, sitting up in bed. Dr. Teal had told him that it was because of his lung tumor that he couldn't sleep lying down. Edward was wondering if he would have to sleep sitting up for the rest of his life. His stomach suddenly felt hollow. / Doris Bell drove along New Hope Road taking back the eight dinner plates her husband had brought over from his aunt's. Doris had said dessert plates and he got dinner plates and she decided just to take them back herself to show him it *could* be done *right*.

"OH, YES, YES," said Mr. Crosley, the mortician. "He's right this way." Why would anybody be coming to see him? he thought.

The girl and woman followed him down the quiet, carpeted hall. "An Annie Jones actually called," he said, "like they asked for in the paper, and said she'd be up here tonight. She wants to see if he's any kin, or any resemblance anyway, she said." Mr. Crosley opened the door, turned on the light. The room was very small, each wall only somewhat longer than the casket against it. One casket open, three closed. "We didn't expect anybody much to come in for a viewing, but we're always prepared. These other caskets are empty." Mr. Crosley stepped back out of the way. He was glad he'd used the casket under the painting — an ocean at sunrise.

"Aren't you a Caldwell?" he asked Alease.

"Yes. I married a Toomey. I'm Alease Toomey, now."

ALEASE FIRST NOTICED that his nose seemed more prominent, more curved than she'd remembered. He was wearing
his wire-rimmed glasses, and—and a black wig. The hair was
longer and less curly than his real hair. "My goodness. He
don't look the same, does he?"

"No he don't," said Cheryl.

Alease saw that Cheryl was ready to cry. "Mr. Crosley, I
actually got to know Mr. Jones fairly well, and I wonder if
Cheryl and me could have just a moment alone."

"Why, of course."

"What about his mustache, Mr. Crosley?" asked Cheryl.
"He had a mustache."

"That was not a real mustache. Gilbert noticed when he
was washing his face. But I'll tell you this. It was not a cheap
mustache. That was one fine fake mustache."

"What about that suit?" asked Cheryl.

"The sheriff brought us that. That actually belonged to
Mr. Jones."

"He did some work for me," said Alease, "and we were
just more or less curious—and were up this way, anyway. I
did get to know him pretty well."

"Certainly," said Mr. Crosley. "I'll be up front. You-all
make yourselves at home. It was a real tragedy. I'm just glad
the right one got shot." He lingered. "It would be a shame to

lose one of the Blaine sisters. What a awful thing. She's a sprightly old soul, idn't she? There was always a difference between them, and she was the sprightly one. If you'd told me one of them was going to shoot a robber, I could have told you which one."

"Excuse me," said a voice at the door. It was Gilbert Allen, another mortician, standing with a short plump woman, dressed up.

"I'm Annie Jones," said the woman. "They put my name in the paper. I'm here to see if I'm some kin to this man. Let me see."

Alease and Cheryl stepped back; Mrs. Jones stepped up. "Well, well," she said. "I honestly thought it could have been Ben, but there ain't no way that there can be Ben, so, I'll just have to say I don't know this one. Ben was bad about changing his name and getting into trouble, so it made sense to me that it might be Ben, and then too, Uncle Bud took out a two-thousand-dollar accidental life insurance policy on every one of them kids, but if it was Ben and he'd had anything, it would have gone to Aunt Shirley and Uncle Bud. Are y'all some kin?" she asked Alease.

"No. We were just neighbors, and we happened to be up here tonight. Had to go to the drugstore, and so we just decided to drop in. He'd done some work for me and I thought he was a right nice man. The way it turned out was a real shock."

"I had to drive fourteen miles, and I'll be glad to get back home and get these shoes off."

A WEEK LATER, Stephen, Terry, and Leland were playing in the dirt with Stephen's toy trucks, by the flower bed.

"My mama," Leland said to Stephen, "said your mama got the murder man to plant flowers for her."

"She did not."

"She said he was hanging around Cheryl too, and she gave him some."

"Some what?"

"Pussy."

"She did not," said Terry.

"She did, too."

"My mama gave him some ice tea one time," said Stephen, "but that was before he done anything wrong." Stephen remembered waking up from his nap at the snap and explosion of the lightning, and going into the kitchen to look for his mama, and then looking out the back window. The rain was pounding down. She was standing in the smokehouse door looking back inside, then turned and looked out into the rain and started running to the house holding a piece of cardboard over her head in one hand and a glass of ice in the other. As she came in from the rain, Stephen saw in through the smoke-house door the faint figure of the man in the yellow shirt. His mother had carried the gypsy man some iced tea for doing work. He remembered how she bounded into the house, dropped the piece of cardboard on the floor, and jumped when she saw Stephen. "You scared me, son. I thought you were asleep." Stephen watched as his mother rinsed off the ice, put it back in the ice tray, added water, and put the ice tray back in the refrigerator freezer. "Did that lightning wake you up?" she had asked him. "Yes ma'am. Why is the gypsy man in the smokehouse?" "He's been doing some work for me. I just took him some tea for the work he'd been doing." She ran her hand through her hair. "We got caught in the rain and had to get in the smokehouse to keep from getting wet."

Leland rammed Terry's toy car with his. "He was trying to kill Miss Blaine," he said, "and if he'd killed her he would have had to go to the electric chair."

"He won't trying to kill her," said Stephen.

"Yes he was."

"No he won't."

"Yes he was."

"No he won't."

They played with the trucks for a while.

"Now Miss Blaine might have to go to the electric chair," said Terry.

"They don't send women to the electric chair," said Leland.

"They do too," said Terry.

"They don't."

"Stephen," called his mother from the back door, "come on in. It's time for your nap. I'll lay down with you."

On the bed she would do what she'd always done. After a few minutes, she'd say, "Now watch my finger. Don't take your eyes off my finger," and she'd hold it up and start moving it in a circle about the size of an egg. Stephen's eyes would follow it. Then she'd say, "Close your eyes and see if you can see it still moving," and he would. "Now open them again," she'd say very softly, and Stephen would, his eyelids heavy.

Soon he'd be asleep and his mother would very quietly get up from the bed and go back into the kitchen to finish her day's work.

BUT ON THIS day, Alease asked June to come over while Stephen slept. With everything else, Raleigh had disappeared again. She needed to get away for a little bit.

She walked toward the blinker light. It had been so long

since she'd taken time to take a walk. She walked by the grocery store, crossed the road, on by the flintrock and down the stretch of road toward the church. Listre Baptist was built when she was a little girl and was for the longest time the biggest building she'd ever seen.

Now about Mr. Jones. How could she have been so fooled? How could she have let something like Mr. Jones happen to her? Something bad could have happened to Stephen. He could have heard things, been influenced in no telling what ways. He could have been shot. All this at the same time he was accepting Jesus.

She looked across the road at the church. Maybe Mr. Crenshaw was in his office.

Then she decided to walk down to the grandstand instead of across the road and into the church.

She thought about Harvey. He was a much better husband than she gave him credit for. He was as loyal and as good a father as she could ever find.

The old grandstand. It had been there when Emmett Odell had jumped up from behind home plate and started running back for a little pop foul ball, had got to running as hard as he could, full speed, looking up at the ball, *wham* into the big corner wood column of the grandstand—full speed, and bounced back unconscious and crumbling. They finally roused him and he went right back and finished the game. And nobody ever forgot it—to this day. And she and Sally Knowles found that half-pack of Lucky Strikes under the grandstand when they were twelve years old and smoked two apiece and then hid the rest.

She looked at the old boarded-up church. "I wonder if the door's open," she said to herself. She could go in and say a prayer for Stephen's safety—a prayer that he might be always safe and able to withstand temptation.

The Stoplights at Hunter's Grove – 2000

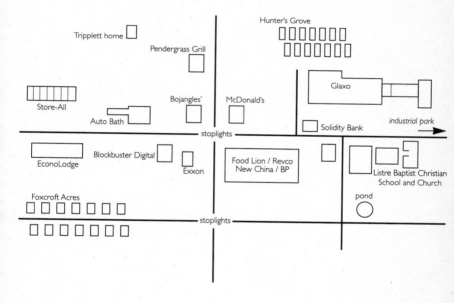

Where Trouble Sleeps
CLYDE EDGERTON

A Reader's Guide

A Conversation with Clyde Edgerton

Q: How did *Where Trouble Sleeps* originate? Is it based on your own experiences?

CE: The story started as a paragraph, a long time ago in my first novel, *Raney*. It was about a little boy sitting on a porch step looking across the road at a service station at an intersection where men were drinking beer. He was upset and delighted at the same time. This paragraph didn't work in *Raney*. I wrote five other novels after *Raney*. But when I started on this present one, I bought a hardback notebook and decided to write scenes from my early childhood.

One of my earliest memories is that of my mother taking me to see the electric chair when I was six years old. She did that to make an impression on me, to ensure that I would not stray in my life and would not succumb to temptation. Because if I did, I would know what would happen. So I decided that it would be a good scene. Also, my mother killed my kitten, Inky, when he got run over. She killed him because there was no chance of his living and she didn't want him to suffer.

Q: Something like losing your kitten when you are six years old, to a baseball bat, is something that you would remember.

CE: Yes, that was a particularly vivid scene in my life—also, watching men drink beer is something that stays with me for some odd reason. I think it's because I was raised in a very religious household. Anyway, I just wanted to write the scenes.

Q: How did you move from just a couple of scenes to a full-blown novel?

CE: I knew if I wrote those scenes—and put them together—I could begin to find out what a story that comes from this time in my life might be like. So, I started, and it was difficult. I knew that I would need a way to fit the scenes together. I needed to see the place where I would be, the place I would be writing about.

When I was growing up I would sit on the front porch of my uncle's grocery store and look across at the men drinking beer. At that intersection there was a blinker light. There were four stores around the blinker light. And there were several other stores and a few houses nearby. So I knew that I had my setting and that all the scenes I had in mind would work here.

Q: **How did you begin to create your characters? How much is based on real people?**

CE: Actually, most of my novels start with a character. In this case, it was the boy sitting on that porch. That six-year-old boy was me, in my memory. But I've also observed six-year-old boys since that time. So, out of my observation, I began to have ideas for this fictional character.

I start out with a character, and I had this character. And I had this character's mother, who, in some ways, initially, was my mother. There's a certain resemblance between my mother and the character who is Alease in the book. So I can draw on what I know and knew about my mother. I can also draw on what I imagine about this fictional character who is Stephen's mother. From my observation, imagination, and experience, I begin to get characters whom I can watch develop.

Q: **What about some of the other characters? What was your inspiration for some of them?**

CE: I knew that I needed to have a character who would make something happen. So what I decided to do was have someone visit this community and stay there for a few days. The best person to visit that I could think of would be some sort of criminal to shake things up a little bit. It so happens that I had written a short story about my version of a misfit, like the one from Flannery O'Connor's story "A Good Man Is Hard to Find." In that story the misfit kills a grandma in a brutal way, and I had come to secretly wish that the grandma could have killed the misfit instead. So, I had decided to write a story about this, and I had this misfit murdered by a grandma—but that was separate from the story about the little intersection with the blinker light. I just decided to put the four and two together—could've been two and two, could've been one and one—and have the misfit show up at my intersection. I decided that I could make up two fictional ladies, based on two ladies I had known in my real life, and one of them would kill this misfit and I knew that right away, very early on.

So, my idea is beginning to come together. I've got a little boy, his mama and this criminal that's going to be murdered and I suddenly decide to just stick that part at the end of the book and I work towards a first draft.

Q: **When you are writing a novel do you consciously have a theme in mind?**

CE: I, on purpose, try not to think much about theme or what this is all about. Although I know, when I finish, that the book needs to be focused in such a way that it is about something in general rather than just a little travelogue or a bunch of incidences that happened in the lives of these people.

About halfway through—about a year into the book—one of the themes that became apparent to me was this whole business of how Stephen's father was pulled away from his mother slightly by his relationship with his brother, Big Steve. At the same time, Alease, Stephen's mother, was being pulled away from Stephen's father by her attention to her brother, Raleigh. I realized that this married couple was being pulled apart because of their loyalty to blood kin. It was exciting to me to think that I could have Stephen, the six-year-old boy, seeing this pulling apart without realizing what he was seeing.

Another theme, I think, centered around the community. It was a community based on very strong cultural and religious norms, running head-on into this stranger in the Buick Eight, who had a different outlook on the way things are and should be.

Q: **You once told me about your use of hypnosis in helping you remember for your writing. Did you use hypnosis in this book?**

CE: Yes, it's true that I used hypnosis to see the past. A few years ago I was in therapy for depression. I do get depressed occasionally, as some of us do.

My hypnosis took place with a psychiatrist who asked me to close my eyes, count to five, and put myself in a setting—a place where I would return to each time I was hypnotized. Now don't leave now. Don't get up and walk out because I'm talking about hypnosis. I used to think the same thing. I thought about somebody holding a little thing in front of you and then you act like a chicken. You run around and squawk like a chicken. But hypnosis can be a kind of relaxation. You know where you are. And it can help you reach in for your unconscious in certain ways. That's what this was about.

In any case, what happened as I drifted off into a hypnotic state was that I returned to that intersection of my childhood, this intersection that was providing the place for my novel. But it focused in on a store that is presently at that intersection. I visualized that place during my first session. That's all I did.

Well, later in hypnosis, I devised a handle on an imaginary telephone pole. And I could pull that handle down and that whole intersection would go back to the way it was in 1950. I saw the store that belonged to my uncle, in real life, the one that my father helped him run. In my mind I turned around, looked across the intersection, and saw my father walk out onto the porch. I started crying, and I cried and cried and cried. It was quite an experience to get back into that intersection.

Q: How did you select the title of the book?

CE: After I had the very last full draft I suddenly realized one day that I didn't have a dog in this book. I thought, for some reason, that I needed a dog. I should have a dog at the service station. Then I had an idea about the dog: where the dog sleeps determines whether or not it will rain that afternoon. Well, by golly, where the dog sleeps will be a good title if I can come up with a good name. For some reason, I had Trombone in my mind—*Where Trombone Sleeps*. Then I got the idea of naming the dog Trouble. *Where Trouble Sleeps*, I decided, would make a good title—and I could connect it to the plot in some way.

Q: **You have a reputation for being a major contemporary southern writer. How do you feel your writing fits into the realm of this literature?**

CE: When I was growing up I didn't know that there was such a thing as southern literature. I knew something about the name Faulkner. But I didn't care. I didn't know. It didn't make any difference to me. Actually, at that time I wanted to fly airplanes, which I ended up doing. But once I was married to Susan Ketchin, she asked if I had read Faulkner. I said no. She told me that I needed to do that. She said, "Have you read O'Connor?" I said no. She said, "Have you read Welty?" I said no.

So I started reading these people and found that they were writing about, in some ways, my past. And I suddenly realized that my past was worthy of fiction, whereas before I always thought I had to be in a war and write about the war. I had to do "heroic" kinds of things before I could write about it. But here were writers writing about similarities to my past in the South. On the other hand, Hemingway, for example, was writing about people in places around the world. And I couldn't quite identify with that. But I could identify with the fiction of these southern writers. So I started writing my own fiction. I soon learned that there was this big subject out there called "southern literature."

Clyde Edgerton Interviews Jack Umstead

The following interview took place on November 13, 1997, at Train's Place, the gas station in this book.

*It's a sunny afternoon in **August 1952**. I approach a bench in front of Train's, where Mr. Umstead—wearing jeans and a yellow shirt—sits.*

(Click—a tape recorder begins recording.)

Edgerton: Do you mind if I sit down?

Umstead: Not at all.

E: My name's Clyde Edgerton. Nice to meet you. I—ah—made you up.

U: Yeah, okay. Whatever the hell that means.

E: I mean, you are a character in a novel I wrote and I've been asked by these people to ask you some questions.

U: I'm just passing through here. I'm visiting some relatives over near T.R. That's about it, as far as I'm concerned. And I don't have but a minute or two. You wrote a novel?

E: I did, and I was wondering if I might ask you a few questions.

U: As long as it's nothing personal. I read some novels one time.

E: One of the characters in this one, the Toomey boy—you know, he sits over there on the grocery steps—grew out of some of my memories about myself and this place.

U: I see. So you're saying . . .

E: That some of what's happening to you now is going in a book. But—no, wait, you don't have to worry about anything. I'm not the law or anything like that. I'll be out of here in just a few minutes. It's pretty complicated. A lot of what's happening to you this week and next is put there by me. I made you up to go in a book. But some of you belongs to just you. Some of you was already there when I found another version of you in a story by another writer. But even so, if it hadn't been for this particular other writer, you would have already been formed to one degree or another when . . .

U: That's crazy. You're crazy.

E: No, wait . . . sit back down, really. I'm not going to turn you in or anything or I already would have. I've got a little tape recorder here in my pocket that will pick up all of this (*sound of recorder being handled, car passing*).

U: That's a nice one. Never seen one like that.

E: I'll tell you what—just let me ask you a few questions. I'll pay this twenty-dollar bill, ask a few questions, and I'll be gone.

U: Don't try anything funny, or I'm gone. Thanks. I can use this.

E: I don't know everything about you, see—I just know enough about you for my book. But the stuff I made up had to fit you. I mean, you were in some sense started by Flannery O'Connor for one of her stories, and in that story you shot a grandmother to death, and then when I put you in my book you started changing some and gradually became someone who only resembled the famous Misfit. Actually, it's more complicated than that and I—

U: I ain't shot no grandmama.

E: You wouldn't remember it.

U: I don't even know you.

E: Let me just tell you a few things I know about you so that you can see that what is happening right this minute is not normal, not in this world we're sitting in—so you can relax. I know you stole that Buick over there. I made that happen. I know you robbed that guy with the zoo in Georgia—six hundred dollars I think it was. I know you're staying in cabin six at the Seattle Inn, right down there. I know you've had a conversation with Cheryl over there at the grill. I know what you said—you asked about her brother and you didn't even know for sure she had a brother. I know you pretended you were Jesus one night down at the church. I made all of that happen in a book and therefore in the heads of readers, but only in the heads of readers, which is where we are right now.

U: What's something I said down there at the church?

E: You recited John 3:16. And I know you were thinking about the front ends of cars the other day—how they look like faces, and all about mental nerves, and I know you noticed the red in Mrs. Toomey's hair.

U: Damnation. Are you God?

E: No. But sometimes I play Him on T.V. In a lot of ways, me and you are in the same racket.

U: Wanna beer?

E: No, thanks. My mother might read this.

U: I'm going to get a beer. Don't go nowhere. (*Creaking bench. Steps. Traffic.*)

E: Umstead has gone inside for a minute. This is working pretty well. He seems interested in talking. I wasn't sure I could get this to work. (*Sounds of footsteps. Creaking bench.*)

U: What's going to happen to me if you know so much?

E: You don't have to worry about that as long as the story stays in print and is read. You have to be alive over and over again, see—for new readers—so even if something bad were to happen to you in the story then you'd have to come back alive. You'll live longer than I do in any case, I hope. My hoping that would mean I'm a writer. An author would want to outlive you. I hope I'm a writer, but sometimes I'm fearful of becoming an author, like when you go on tour or write about yourself while pretending to write about something else. There's a danger of that here. There are eight "I's" in this paragraph. Make that nine.

U: I mean what happens to me in the books then?

E: I'd just as soon not talk about that. Well, here, let me cut the recorder off. (*Click.*) (*Click.*)

U: . . . and I get to change with whoever's reading the book.

E: Right, for example, I've had a woman say she fell in love with you. I had another say you were the personification of evil. I even had a guy, a radio interviewer, wonder if there was some sort of "gender problem" with you—he wondered if you might be a woman.

U: A woman! Where the hell did he come up with that?!

E: It had something to do with your fake mustache and what somebody said to you. I don't think he read . . .

U: Who was the woman fell in love with me? You think you could get her here somehow?

E: No, I couldn't do that . . .

U: You can't just write her here?

E: No. And I don't mean you completely change with different readers. You keep doing the same stuff.

U: So you caused all that with Cheryl down in my cabin?

E: Sort of. You both had some say in that, I think.

U: You ever watch any dirty movies?

E: What?

U: You ever watch any dirty movies? *(Click) (Click)* . . . are you? I had a hard life growing up, man. I had bad stuff happen to me and then I get up here among these people and there's something ain't fair about most of what's going on. It just ain't fair. Why come I should have to bust my ass to go straight and have jerks like #8#%*@# come in here in his big Cadillac and with his big diamond ring and he's doing all the same stuff I'm doing—but in his mind. I know he is.

E: I made him up too. But I don't know everything about his mind. His mind is . . .

U: Wait a minute, I ain't finished. And I ain't got no mind I can do stuff in all that much. I have to act it out. That's my problem, I have to act it out and since I have to act it out, I have to act it out. It was YOU putting all that stuff in my head. I could tell it was coming from somewhere. I didn't put it there. You did. I got along okay until that stuff starts coming in my head and then I just have to ACT IT OUT. So you're the one that's been . . . you're the one that makes me have to . . .

E: Wait a minute. Waaaait a minute. You don't have a bad life. I mean, as a character. There's a lot of good about your life. You get to travel. You got a new car. You get to listen to music. You can't just do what you want to, or else you wouldn't be a character in a novel.

U: Yeah, well . . . (*tractor passing*) I don't know. I do have some pretty good days. Could you get that woman fell in love with me here somehow?

E: I can't. She might can. See that light pole over there? Let me tell you something. The way this novel got started was, I was seeing a psychiatrist for depression and I was hypnotized and—

U: You jumped around like a chicken.

E: Weelllll tttttthhhhaaaaatttt'ssss aaaa kkiinnnddd ooooffff . . . (*dead battery—no AA batteries were available so I was unable to record the rest of the interview which was mostly about different makes and models of American automobiles. The Korean War and religion were also discussed—briefly.*)

Originally printed in *The North Carolina Review of Books*.

Reading Group Questions
and Topics for Discussion

1. How would you characterize Stephen's relationship with each of his parents? With his church and his religion?

2. What prospects of stability are offered to the community by the church? Instability?

3. How is the church important to Jack Umstead?

4. How is the setting (1950s, rural community) important to the story?

5. What might Alease see in Jack Umstead and why? Does he have any redeeming qualities? If so, what are they?

6. Discuss the significance of the title.

7. How are the major characters and the community changed by Umstead's visit?

8. How does shifting point of view aid or hinder your reading of this story?

9. How might a year-2000 visit by Jack Umstead to Listre, North Carolina, be different from the 1952 visit in *Where Trouble Sleeps*?

10. How were your childhood views of God and religion different from those of Stephen?

11. How will Stephen's experiences as a child in *Where Trouble Sleeps* influence his life as an adolescent? As an adult? Which of the adults in the novel will he most resemble as an adult?

12. What events or experiences in your own childhood could become the basis for a novel?

ABOUT THE AUTHOR

While he was growing up in North Carolina, probably no one would have predicted that CLYDE EDGERTON would be a professional writer. Most would have placed bets on his being a baseball player or a rock musician, even though his parents thought he might be a missionary or a concert pianist. He loved to hunt and fish with buddies. But even without early signs of literary leanings, Clyde has become one of the most prominent contemporary writers. Even though he is a product of the South, drawing primarily from one segment of society, his insight into the human condition makes his work universal.

With degrees from the University of North Carolina at Chapel Hill, he has taught writing and English education at various colleges and universities. He is very much in demand as a speaker about the writing process and as a reader of his own fiction. Clyde continues to write in Orange County, North Carolina, where he lives with his wife, Susan, and daughter, Catherine.

Praise for Clyde Edgerton

"Clyde Edgerton is an American Treasure."

—*San Diego Union-Tribune*

Raney

"A funny, deft, heartening book. If I were single, I'd marry it."

—Roy Blount, Jr.

"Not since Huckleberry Finn has there been a character like Raney."

—*Dallas Times Herald*

In Memory of Junior

"This is Edgerton in top form, cracking the dialect and whomping the language. . . . The tales flip and twist, leap and flash like hooked fish in the kind of rollicking black humor that only Clyde Edgerton can write."

—*Greensboro News & Record*

"Wonderfully outlandish."

—*Entertainment Weekly*"

Killer Diller

"Will make you laugh until your sides hurt."

—*Atlanta Journal & Constitution*

"Edgerton's books are suffused with perfect pitch, with the right tone, voice and tempo . . . Readers unfamiliar with Edgerton should treat themselves"

—*The Boston Globe*

Walking Across Egypt

"Reading this book is like sitting down to a big round table full of the best food you ever put in your mouth, you can't quit eating for a minute, this is just so good."

—Lee Smith

"An unpretentious, finely crafted novel that will linger with the readers like the last strains of a favorite hymn. It is more enjoyable than a pitcher full of sweet tea and one of Mattie's home-cooked dinners."

—*The Atlanta Journal*

The Floatplane Notebooks

"Edgerton has written a novel beyond our imagination. It belongs next to the family Bible. It belongs in your memory, and quickly. The sheer joy, and restorative powers of the novel, are like no other book that I can think of."

—Rick Bass for *The Houston Post*

"So perfect is the author's control that each voice, like an individual bell in a handbell choir, rings true."

—Barbara Kingsolver for *The New York Times Book Review*